The Sled Dog

A Sheridan County Mystery

Erin Lark Maples

LODESTAR
LITERARY

To all the very good dogs,
Lily & Daisy, most of all.

1

ACH OF THE TINY, twinkling lights held a memory for Elizabeth. The electric strands were wrapped around light
poles, trees, and every vertical surface on Main Street. She
wanted to reach out and pinch each bulb. Give them a twist,
lock in the cheery glow. "Aren't they beautiful?"

Some store fronts used the traditional reds and greens in
their decoration. This classic duo signaled a huge tree as the
centerpiece in a cookie cutter world. Magazine spread-wor-
thy dinner tables, a complete and present family.

Yellows were starlight and good cheer. A second bottle of
champagne. The warm whites were their cousins, anchored
by a stiff aunt, silver wrapping paper, and an office holiday
party. Each of these hues flattered the skin, a head thrown
back in laughter, sparkles in their eyes as the countdown to
midnight comes to a close.

Blues hummed, a complex glow. A depth of melancholy, an
undercurrent of sadness that permeated her childhood. The
cold, wintry depths of Lake Union. Family would dissipate
from forced togetherness as soon as acceptable. Father to the
living room, camped out in front of the television. Mother to
the back porch, raining or not, to smoke the single, annual
cigarette. Casey never minded time in his room by himself.
Only Elizabeth held the loss in her lap, the idea of what a
family should be.

This year, Elizabeth clung to her favorite hue, the purples.
The color of keeping a strong back through life's curve balls,
your chin high. Magenta, violet, and aubergine are colors for a

queen. Come what may, this was Elizabeth's first holiday season in Sheridan County. She would claim it for herself, make it a success. Purple was determination, worthiness, strength.

Her son stretched a fingertip toward a tiny bulb, curious. He too, picked purple.

Holidays were a mix of feelings for Elizabeth. How would they be for Rhett? The two-year old was content to observe the world around him. The lights reflected in his eyes, played in streaks through his dark hair.

He twisted in his stroller toward the window display. An arrangement of wooden farm animals circled a makeshift corral. The animals inhabited a matching wooden barn, painted red and white. Rhett pressed a palm against the glass.

"I see it, buddy. Even the little ducks are adorable." Near the barn door stood a figure with a straw hat, overalls, and painted-on boots. The farmer, on guard. Elizabeth cocked her head. "He looks a bit like Uncle Casey, don't you think?"

Elizabeth ducked her head to peer below the glass shelf on which the toys were displayed. She craned her neck to view the price tag.

Multiple digits and more than she'd planned to spend. *Shoot.*

Elizabeth bit her bottom lip, reconsidered the expense, then shook her head. Too early to know how far her paycheck would need to stretch.

"Everyone is getting socks this year," she said to Rhett. "No matter which holiday they celebrate."

Her son only had eyes for the trio of white and gray sheep huddled in a cluster. A sheep dog stood guard nearby, a permanent vigil.

"We'd better let Santa know you have a wish list." *And by Santa, I mean Margery Hart.* The woman had all the money in the world and no family to spend it on, as she liked to say. Between Marg and her neighbors, Rhett had more honorary grandparents than cattle on the prairie.

Elizabeth pushed on the handle of the stroller. Rhett strained to see the now beloved toy set as it disappeared behind them.

"Let's see what's in the other windows. I bet they are full of more surprises."

People flowed past them on the sidewalk. Many smiled at Rhett. People cooed over his sweater, a gift from Elizabeth's ex-mother-in-law. Elizabeth chafed at each compliment. The sweater was one of a half dozen sent, wrapped in tissue, in a name-brand box. A winter wardrobe caliber Elizabeth could never afford.

"Maybe they'll sell me just the sheep," she whispered under her breath as they continued the walk under the soft glow of streetlights.

A roving band of carolers paused outside the jewelers and serenaded those nearby. At the next block, a row of white tents held carafes of hot chocolate, sleigh rides, and kettle corn. Others held vendors of knitted hats, handmade jewelry, and cherry wood carving boards. Sheridan welcomed residents with the promise of a merry season.

Main Street was aided by vintage buildings rich in charm and decorative accents. People from across the county bundled up to crowd the sidewalks and shops in search of the perfect gift and enjoy the company. At dusk, the mayor flipped the switch at the courthouse that lit several conifers and started a ripple effect down the street as the businesses followed suit. To a gal from Seattle, this was a picturesque heaven.

Light the Night was held each Saturday after Thanksgiving. Turkey and cranberries packed away, residents left their homes in all but the most inclement weather to secure a bag of just-roasted chestnuts.

Elizabeth forked over a few dollars in exchange for a warm paper sack. She cracked open one of the blackened shells and handed a cooled piece to Rhett before popping the rest in her mouth.

Thanksgiving had been good. Delicious. A party. They'd dined at the Hart Ranch. Ten people around a table heaped with ham, green beans, and a caramel-colored pumpkin pie. The bounty came from local farmers, including Casey's goat cheese baked in a quiche. Elizabeth had brewed a special winter ale for the event, with hints of orange zest and spruce. Marg had a second pint and proclaimed the meal a success.

Elizabeth couldn't remember the last table at which so many had gathered together. If Blau Family gatherings were a disaster, holidays with Nick had been a show of catered, pre-packaged meals bought in haste from an upscale market. Seats at their sparse table were more institutional than welcoming.

Last night, she saw delight in her brother's face when Randall's smoked turkey was followed by Marg who hefted a smaller roast of faux meat. A vegetarian, her brother was happy to receive the treat. Along with her ale, Elizabeth brought a mammoth pumpkin cheesecake. She'd used her experimental ale in the batter and grated orange zest into the graham cracker crust. The result was a silky smooth concoction. Marg proclaimed it the foundation of a future restaurant.

Elizabeth dared to hope. She'd wanted something along those lines, a place of her own.

In the aftermath of the violent beginning to her residence as the Banner School teacher, she'd dreamed of an escape. The school board decided to close the school for the remainder of the year. Elizabeth had been redistributed to the school in Story, her students bussed elsewhere.

The board cobbled together a position in which she was part librarian, part reading teacher, part playground monitor. She'd come to love the residents of Story as she got to know their children.

"Hey, Lizard-breath. Little nephew. How's it going?" Her brother Casey bounced up and down inside his booth, blowing on his hands as he kept his feet moving.

"This is all so...precious." Elizabeth gestured at the tents, the lights, the people. "I feel like an extra on one of those family channel movies. How's business?"

"Folks are going nuts for the rosemary and cracked pepper. The huckleberry, too. The case of crackers I ordered is gone, and people are buying up all the honey I brought." Her brother's cheese business had taken off in the last few months thanks to some new distribution deals and the word-of-mouth from well-known neighbors. He owned a goat farm on a sizable spread, and his artisan cheese was drawing a solid fan base.

Casey's ranch was their home now, too. At least for the time being. The ranch had become her son's favorite place, and she wanted him to enjoy it. She knew better than most that having so many people who cared for you in one place was a gift.

A family approached the tent, and Casey shifted into business mode. With a wave, they moved on.

Thanksgiving had been good to their family. Looming, though, was the new year. Nick, Rhett's father, would take Rhett back to Seattle for a week. Elizabeth was doing her best to ignore the upcoming separation.

Collar drawn up against the weather, Elizabeth tugged at Rhett's corduroy coat. Darkness had fallen an hour ago. Light flakes dusted his hair, and she dropped two kisses on his rosy cheeks. When she tucked the blanket tighter at his sides, he reached out to her for a hug. She snuggled him into her arms. The cheerful glow of a familiar window beckoned Elizabeth inside with its promised warmth.

"It may just be you and me, little buddy," she said to the cuddly boy in her arms. "But we make a pretty good team. Let's get you out of the cold."

A few streets away, another body shivered, alone and vulnerable.

2

SNOWFLAKE CUTOUTS PAPERED THE inside of the many-paned window. Inside Beans & Biscuits, the rafters were strung with more snowflakes. Even the bakery cases were dressed for the season. Silver foil doilies under the trays of pastries in the glass fronted case reflected light from within. Enid, the owner of Elizabeth's favorite coffee shop, kept her business open for this special evening event. She'd gone all out.

Enid and her employee Gary, the shop's full-time barista and town gossip, worked like elves to fill the case with cookies, brownies, and danishes. They'd pored over every cookbook they could find to represent as many winter holidays as they could fit in the case. There were jam-filled Polish kolaczki, melomakarona from Cyprus, and powdered reganadas from Mexico.

"Who would complain about more sweets?" As a kid, Enid's house rule was that all arguments were worked out over a cup of tea and a cookie. She took this upbringing to heart and then some at the holidays.

Enid packed cookies into takeaway bags and boxes behind the counter. With gloved hands and tongs, she selected macarons, pizzelles, and rugelach to fill a customer's order. Gary did brisk business behind the mammoth espresso machine. A whiz behind the steamer, he pulled shots of espresso to combine with milks and syrups in various concoctions. Enid and Gary served lines that were several revelers deep. The shop hummed with the sound of people exclaiming over the offerings at Beans that night.

Elizabeth joined the cue and tucked the narrow stroller as far against the pastry case as she could. The shop was warm, and laughter filled the space to the rafters.

The high school art club had prints for sale along the walls. Enid loved to turn the shop into a makeshift gallery for the students. Customers sipped mugs of hot cocoa and nibbled slices of pumpkin bread as they checked out the artwork.

Rhett's eyes never left the trays of cookies at stroller-level. Elizabeth crouched down to take in his perspective. The oversized silver bell above the shop door jangled as someone entered and joined the line behind them.

"No clue how I'm supposed to make up my mind with all of this going on. It's nothing short of cruel. This much temptation in a twenty-foot radius should be illegal." Josephine Wolf, career volunteer and the wife of one of the county sheriffs, removed her pom-pom-topped beanie and fluffed her hair. A few gray strands caught in the light. "I'll be sure to complain to the council. Can't have these kinds of shenanigans. This is a family place."

Elizabeth smiled and stood to greet her friend.

Enid called from her perch behind the counter, "I heard that, Jo."

Jo tugged her knitted hat back down over her ears and stooped to greet Rhett. "How's our little cowboy doing?"

The little boy pointed at the display of endless cookies in case Jo had yet to see their glory.

A customer at the counter leaned over the counter to address Gary. "You'd better get on out there, Gary. I mean, it's not like you have a chance this year or any year with that rig you've brought, but you owe it to your dad to at least make an effort. I'm told not all of us can live up to the family name. Losing with dignity is your next best bet."

"Advice noted. Can I get you some caffeine for the road?" Gary rested both wrists on the counter, meeting the customer's eyes. His tone implied that a to-go order was the only option.

"Americano," the source of the gruff voice replied, his broad back toward Elizabeth. His bulky frame was shrouded in a black jacket, a black Stetson perched on his head. She didn't recognize this man, but didn't want to, either.

Gary slid the drink across the counter and accepted a stack of bills. "You know where to find the sugar, seems you're short on sweetness."

"Funny guy. See you out there. Not that anyone would notice if you were gone. Me, on the other hand—." The man picked up his cup and left the snug shop.

Elizabeth whispered to Jo, "Who was that?"

Jo pursed her lips and shook her head. "Someone who's had it easy for far too long."

"Surprised his ego fit through that door," Enid muttered. "Welcome in, y'all. Thanksgiving go well?"

Elizabeth recounted details from her meal, including the multitude of sauces and sides.

"So you all clearly suffered at Marg Hart's table. Dang. I need to land an invite next year."

"There's room at that table. It's huge!"

"Ah, well, I'll be in Florida come next fall if things go my way. Just have to convince Gary here to hold down the fort, feed the cats. Speaking of pets, I have a special cookie I decorated just for Rhett. Give me a sec to grab it from the back." Enid untied her apron, hung it on a hook, and ducked into her office off the little hallway to the back of the shop.

While they waited, Elizabeth perused the latte menu, a habit without purpose. Most days, Gary was halfway through preparing her usual before she stepped up to the counter. Tonight was different. Special. Elizabeth wanted to savor the evening. New traditions called for new beverages.

"You're considering something new," Gary said. "How about peppermint? It's homemade syrup..."

"Sold. Hot chocolates. 'Tis the season and all. Make it two, please."

Gary scribbled the order across two paper cups, then spooned a thick, dark chocolate syrup into each. He poured milk into the metal carafe and nestled it under the steamer wand. "Cold out there."

"Getting more so by the minute. Mostly dry though." In a place like Wyoming, some days, winter whipped up out of thin air, like a visit from an unwanted relative. "How was your turkey day?"

"We did it right. Mom got to keep her feet up all day, and my brother didn't start a fire with the deep fried turkey." Gary poured foamy milk into the rich, thick chocolate sauce he'd spooned into each of the cups. He slid the cups across the counter, and the aroma of peppermint wafted her way.

Enid returned with a cookie on a square of waxed paper. Cut from a ginger dough, the animal shape had been decorated with white and gray piping, a face so dark brown it was almost black, and a yellow stripe for a collar complete with a nonpareil stand-in for a miniature bell. She held it out to Rhett.

This was a perfect rendition of a sheep not unlike the ones he'd coveted in the window display. There weren't any sheep at Casey's place, but they'd discovered a flock down the lane. After introductions, their neighbor had invited Rhett to come by anytime.

Elizabeth brought diced pumpkin chunks for the woolies during their last visit. One ewe, distracted by the orange cubes, ignored the two-year-old human running his fingers through her wool and pressing his cheek to her warm belly.

They'd come by Beans for a treat afterward. Elizabeth had updated Enid and Gary about Rhett's new adoration and had called Jo when she got home.

Elizabeth's son had yet to say his first word. She and everyone who loved the sweet little boy clung to any new display of interest in hopes he would soon be motivated to talk about it. Her ex, Rhett's father, considered the delay all the more reason for Rhett (with or without Elizabeth) to move back to Seattle where specialists could poke and prod him into development. Elizabeth disagreed. This was Rhett's home now. Being around the animals at farms and ranches brought a light to his eyes they couldn't replicate in a big city.

"You are an incredible artist. This is too pretty to eat!"

"Gary and I were here a bit late last night. We opened a pinot and went to town with the piping bags." Enid waved her hand over the top of the case where the sugar cookies held court. Everything from a Yule log to a host of people in multicolored sweaters and scarves lined the prominent shelf. "Got a little creepy here that late. Lots of ghosts on Main Street, you know. Anyway, we got to bed early enough to finish the lot of them this morning. Take your pick. It's on the house."

Elizabeth peered again at the shapes below where her breath fogged the glass. She selected a delicate snowflake. Each bend and angle mirrored the next. The cookie was iced with a thin layer of pale blue and dusted with edible, silver dust that sparkled in the light.

"Thank you. I need to get used to seeing these everywhere." Wyoming winter weather made Elizabeth nervous. The temperate Pacific Northwest was nothing compared with the arctic air that would dip down from the pole toward the plains states.

"So far," Gary said. "Snowiest month can be December but it is just as often March."

"I'll tuck that nugget up here," she said, and tapped the crown of her head. "You keep threatening me with a trivia night after the holidays. I've got to study up."

Elizabeth loved trivia. It was a big part of why she made a passable science teacher and a decent homebrewer. Knowing facts, being able to rely on solid information, gave her a sense of comfort, security. On the nights when her parents fought and Casey escaped to a friend's house, she'd read everything in the house from cover to cover to drown out the shouting. Encyclopedias, fashion magazines, appliance manuals. Her head was full of figures, directions, and elucidations. When she was nervous, she'd retreat into the lists of details that shaped the moment, often spouting off facts to cover her anxiety. Nine days out of ten, it was a useless ability. Gary promised she'd be a ringer at trivia nights at a local bar.

Elizabeth claimed a tiny table near the window. She maneuvered the stroller into the spot next to her chair and handed Rhett the sheep. He stared at the confection in wonder for almost a minute before sticking one leg in his mouth and snapping it off with a tentative bite. As he chewed, his face lit up with joy. Elizabeth sampled her own cookie and mirrored his expression. Buttery, crisp, and balanced in sweetness, the cookie was a triumph.

Jo pulled up another chair and joined them. She'd selected a ginger palm tree, its fronds edged in green piping. It was part of Enid's Future in Florida collection, the baker explained.

Her friend unwrapped an eggplant scarf from around her neck. "I'll have to brush my teeth twice tonight. Worth it, though."

"Speaking of worth it, how was Nebraska?"

"My mother used to say that every place has its beauty, but a couple days with Clint's family, after a couple decades of marriage, and I'm still trying to figure out the draw of that cornstalk-covered flatland. I had nothing else to do for the last ten hours but stare out the window at the ironed-out nothing that is the center of our county." Jo cracked off the trunk of the palm tree and took a bite. "First time Clint's had more than three days off to rub together in far too long, so there was that."

"You're a good wife."

"Eh, he's a good man. We don't get out there often, and it wasn't exactly torture. Doesn't kill me to go now and again, does it?"

"Life's too short."

"Indeed. What are you drinking? Gary was fuming from that blowhard, so I didn't want to tax him with my usual." Jo's drink orders were second only in complexity to her Christmas shopping list.

"Ask Gary for something with peppermint. It's the latest trend."

"Roger that. How about an extra napkin for our cookie monster while I'm at it?" Jo wiped at Rhett's crumb-covered lips and crumpled the napkin into her hand. She got to her feet and headed to the register to order.

The woman had not only become Elizabeth's closest friend in the last few months but was also Rhett's babysitter. Jo and Clint didn't have any children of their own and were ersatz parents for many. Jo refused to take any money, said the toddler fix was therapy. The woman's support was worth its weight in gold to Elizabeth.

They finished their snacks, cleaned up the table, and bundled back up.

"Ready to walk?" Jo brought out a donkey figurine from deep within a jacket pocket and handed it to Rhett. "Looks just like Bessie, doesn't it?"

He gripped the sturdy plastic animal, turning it in his hands.

They pushed out the door after a wave to Enid and Gary. The lines hadn't slowed. If anything, business picked up, as though a crescendo were coming.

Out on the street, they began to stroll. A few people had given up the walk and plunked themselves down in lawn chairs under awnings.

Her hands in her pockets, Jo smiled at sidewalk passersby. "Any news?"

"Well, Nick was right about one thing. There aren't any specialists here. I am going to have to take him to Billings."

Jo nodded. "Let me know when, and I'll go with you."

Elizabeth had made a deal with Nick that if Rhett had not started to talk by two, she would take him to see a specialist. "Nick is pressing me to take him to Seattle."

"But you're not going back."

"No. I'm not going back."

"But you're worried."

The words grated on Elizabeth's conscience, but she had to be honest with Jo. She heaved a sigh that sent a puff of warm air into the night. "I'm worried." How could a mother not be?

"Give them a call in Billings. See what they say. I'm sure you can get his records from the Emerald City sent out here. I'm told we even have computers in some medical offices."

Elizabeth gave her a wry smile. Then, she took a deep breath and said, "You know, he's going to be with Nick for Christmas. In Seattle."

"How do you feel about that?"

"I want him to have a healthy relationship with his father. And I'm freaked out. Basically those two, opposing thoughts are wrestling in my mind, nonstop."

"Sounds exhausting. You need a distraction."

Jo paused behind a couple in a pair of lawn chairs. They were bundled up to their chins and traded a thermos of what smelled like tomato soup between them.

"What are all these people waiting for?"

"My dear friend, welcome to your first Mushers Parade."

3

"MUSHERS—AS IN SLEDS AND dogs and miles and miles of snowy trails?"

"A time-honored holiday tradition here in beautiful Sheridan, Wyoming. Teams from all over come to Main Street to show off their teams. All in preparation for the big race, of course."

"Race?"

"The Sheridan County Sled Run."

They paused at the corner of Main and Works until the crosswalk sign cycled in their favor. In the distance, the faint sound of bells jangled.

"I had no idea sled races were a thing outside Alaska. Tell me more."

"I'll let the dogs themselves do the talking. Here they come." Jo pointed south toward the courthouse. The source of the ringing bells came into view.

Atop a mammoth sled with red rails and pulled by a team of dogs wearing antlers stood Santa Claus. He held on with one hand and waved at the crowd with the other.

"Santa is a musher?" Elizabeth rubbed her hands together as she watched the spectacle unfold along the main thoroughfare of the town. As Santa grew closer, Elizabeth recognized the square jaw and broad brow of the person beneath the wig and beard. His eyes twinkled as his sleigh passed by.

"Is that...?"

Gary drove the ersatz reindeer team past the trio. The barista, decked out in a stuffed red and white suit with a matching hat, waved at Rhett and winked in Elizabeth's direction.

"Sure is," Jo said. "His family is a long line of mushers. Two brothers and three sisters. He's a little less competitive than most of them, but as Gary says, they're back in Fairbanks."

Close behind the makeshift North Pole sleigh came the other teams. Riders stood on the solid base of their sleds, knees slightly bent, all focus on their dogs. Each followed the team in front of them, a careful orchestration. Spectators kept a respectful distance. Awe flooded the crowd as the power slid by on display.

Rhett watched with big eyes that twinkled with delight. Elizabeth hefted him up into her arms so he could see above the heads. "What is all this?"

"Before the race, teams that live close enough participate in the parade to show off their dogs and get everyone excited for the upcoming event."

The dogs were focused forward in spite of the jumping, cheering, and clapping of the crowds gathered on the sidewalk.

"Rhett sure loves it," Elizabeth said. His mouth hung open in awe at a sled that held a driver dressed up like an elf. She stretched on tiptoe to assess the number of teams in line. "I didn't even know they could drive on asphalt."

"There won't be any drag racing, that's for sure."

The next team was color-coordinated, each dog sporting a green or white bowtie. One of the dogs yipped, and Rhett clapped his hands together, the donkey sandwiched between his fingers.

"You might have a future musher on your hands," Jo said with a smile.

"I'm pretty sure he's going to need his own zoo at this rate. He's yet to find an animal he doesn't love."

Another sled brought cheers from the crowd. This one was decked out with flashing lights, a speaker blasting Christmas songs, and a ragtag bunch of animals hauling its bulk. The driver was dressed like Frosty the Snowman and tossed peppermints to the kids who lined the sidewalks. One smacked against Elizabeth's jacket, and Frosty called out an apology.

Elizabeth laughed as she plucked the treat from her pocket and waved. "Don't take this the wrong way but some seem more...focused than others."

"Eh, for some, it's a hobby. They're here for fun, the fresh air, camaraderie. For others, it's a serious sport. Heavy competition. A lot of these people grew up with families who had dog teams. Competed on the regular. This race gives them a chance to relive some glory days."

Elizabeth looked to the sled behind Frosty. The musher was bedecked in head-to-toe snow gear, along with thick gloves. They smiled and waved, yet their attention was on their pack. Eight dogs trotted in unison, a ripple of motion pulling the sled down the street. This was a fun event, but the focus of participants belied a serious edge of competition. "When you say race, what exactly are we talking about?"

"Oh, nothing like the Iditarod or any of the other distance races. Competitors have a few options. The Run starts at five miles and tops out at a twelve-mile trail. Drivers pick their competitive level. New Year's Day on the mountain top, rain or shine."

"Is it dangerous?"

"To a degree. But there are rules and regs to keep people and the dogs safe. Folks come from all the way up in Alaska to participate. A few from Canada, Idaho, and the Dakotas drive out. People wouldn't come if it wasn't a legit race."

Next up was a team that pulled a sleek, dark sled with silver railing. All of the straps, collars, and even the booties each dog wore were the same shade of midnight with polished metal fittings. The driver, too, wore black. Elizabeth could make out a stern brow, piercing blue eyes, and tight lips but not much more from her place in the crowd. On the chest of their jacket and across the side of the sled was the same silver, stylized dog silhouette. A speaker tucked inside the sled played metal music as the team sped by.

"Black Dogs," Jo said. Before Elizabeth could prod, she continued, "That's Bobby Black. He and his brother, Winton, raise champion sled dogs. Pretty well-known in the sport."

Elizabeth was no expert on canine superiority, but she knew a capable animal when she saw one. Let alone eight. "Those are some good-looking dogs."

"Good-looking and winners. Their team annihilates the competition, time after time. But then again, for them, it's a business."

"Makes sense." Elizabeth watched the straight back of Bobby pass them on his sled. What must it be like to stand for hours on that tiny platform? Mushers were tough. "If you're going to breed championship dogs, you have to win championships."

The final sled, a curvy wooden structure that was more gingerbread style than aerodynamics, was pulled by a donkey. She wore a sash across her side that read Course Master. Astride the wooden sled was a familiar face.

Clint Wolf blew his wife a kiss as he passed. The crowd cheered their Sheriff's run, courtesy of Bessie.

Elizabeth, wide-eyed, mouth agape, turned to Jo. "Explanation, please!"

A sheepish Jo held her hands out. "Surprise? I didn't want to say anything in case it didn't turn out. We had no idea if a donkey would be up for it, but she took to it like a...well, uh..."

"Husky to snow?"

Jo laughed. "Yeah. We had a back-up plan that he'd ride with Santa if she got crowd-shy."

"Looks to me like she loved it."

The she in question, Bessie, had been adopted by the Wolfs a few months earlier.

"That was the end of it," Jo said, as the people gathered began to thin out, heading for their cars. "Want to say hi to Clint before we leave?"

Rhett craned his head to check for more teams. He hadn't taken his eyes off the parade since it started. "Rhett votes yes."

They headed down Brooks Street toward the park where an array of trailers parked. Each was attached to a pickup truck. Everywhere, there were dogs in various states of travel preparation. The barking was deafening at times. Rhett held his hands over his ears when a howl kicked up among them.

Gary, still in Santa attire, chatted with another driver. Red velvet hat in hand, the faux beard hung below his chin. When he saw Rhett, he yanked the beard back up over his face.

"Santa," Jo said. "We thought we might find you back here. Taking down a naughty and nice list for the dogs?"

"Ho, ho, hello," Gary said. He bent down toward Rhett in the stroller. "Well, hello there, young man. I see you've been taking good care of a friend." Gary pointed to the plastic donkey wedged against the side of the stroller. "I'll be sure to let the elves know."

"That was incredible," Elizabeth said to Gary. "I had no idea all of this happened here. It's seriously impressive!"

"Thanks. My father and brothers were race winners. I'm just a casual tourist compared to them. This guy, though" —Gary clapped his hand on the shoulder of the man standing next to him—"he's the real deal."

The man, his face obscured by a shaggy beard, extended his hand to Elizabeth. The same emblem as was on the Black Dog sled was on this man's jacket as well. Unlike the musher, this man had eyes the gray of a sky about to snow. "Winton Black. Gary is too kind."

"Elizabeth Blau. I don't think Gary could be anything less. I saw your sled out there. Those are some serious looking dogs."

"Gary's not the only one with a competitive brother," Winton said. "Speaking of brothers, though, we need to finish loading up and head back up the mountain, so I'd better find Bobby. Nice to meet you, Elizabeth. Take it easy, Jo." He gave them a half wave and headed out through the maze of people and dogs toward the other trailers.

"If you're looking for Clint," Gary said, "he was in the event tent."

"Poor man can't ever avoid bureaucracy," Jo said.

They wound their way through those who scrambled to pack away sleds and dogs. Many of the dog handlers waved at Rhett as they passed.

Dogs were everywhere. Most were leashed up in some fashion, though a few wandered free. There were more varieties, shapes, and sizes than she could have pictured. In her mind, a sled dog was a fluffy husky, with blue eyes and a single-syllable name. In the crates that filled the trailers and in packs around the vehicles, she saw dog breeds she didn't recognize. Colors ranged from black to brownish to reddish to yellow. Some were bulky with muscle, and others looked like distance runners. Many crates had names affixed to the front, metal placards with names like Trixie, Bartholomew, Ryder, and Max.

The Black Dogs van was parked parallel to the sidewalk. Van and trailer matched the sled, the Black Dogs emblem on each side. Several dog handlers scrambled around the animals, brushing coats, checking paws, and hustling them into crates. Each crate was black metal wire with black, padded bedding in the bottom. Elizabeth could hear the tension of an argument, two voices bickering, from among the caretakers. When they passed the end of the van, she could see Winton and Bobby with barely a foot of space between them. Winton stood with hands on his hips, shaking his head, eyes on the asphalt. Bobby pointed a finger in his brother's face, shouting. A large, wolf-like dog wound itself around Winton's legs. It was difficult to pick out sounds in the general din, but Elizabeth thought the dog emitted a low growl when Bobby jabbed his finger against Winton's chest.

"This is *not* what we agreed to."

Winton met his brother's stare. "Where is she?"

"I have no idea. Now stick to the subject at hand, this is serious!"

"I'm not going to apologize for doing what's right."

Bobby dropped his hand and took two steps away from his brother. He threw his arms up in the air and then stomped back over to Winton. "Everything we've worked for, everything *I've* worked for, means nothing to you?"

Elizabeth missed the end of the argument. She couldn't stay without becoming an obvious eavesdropper.

She, Jo, and Rhett approached a white tent, anchored between two vehicles with guylines. Clint Wolf leaned over a sheaf of documents, sliding his finger down the top page. A woman held a laptop open with a spreadsheet on the screen. The two checked data between the two sources. Clint rubbed at his chin.

"How's our Course Master holding up?"

"Hello, my lovely bride. Hello, neighbors." He reached across the table to give Rhett a high five. "How was the show from the stands?"

"Fantastic," Elizabeth said. "You're looking at Sheridan County's newest big fan of dog sledding."

"Glad to hear it," Clint said. "For a lot of people, this is a tradition. We're about five years in on hosting our own race, but there are many all over from which people can choose. Around the northern parts, it's popular for a reason."

"Rhett loved it, too. I'm only bummed he won't be here for the race." Elizabeth thought of her promise to Nick. She'd thought it would be easy this year since she was new and didn't know what Rhett would be missing.

"We won't be too much longer. What if you go check out the teams?"

"Wouldn't kill us to look at some adorable pups, that's for sure."

4

MANY OF THE SLEDDING operations had exited the makeshift parking lot and headed for home. A few still loaded their vehicles or lingered with their peers, leaning against their trucks and chatting.

One group, from Ontario, had an all female crew, dogs and humans. All of them, dogs included, were decked out in bright purple. Bundled up for the drive, the women wore matching knit sweaters and hats. The canines they brushed and snuggled were decked out in matching collars.

"Would your little boy like to pet one? Our girls are super sweet—for the most part. Buttons is one of the sweetest pups we have." A woman in a snowflake scarf approached, a dog at her side. She held a giant coffee cup in one hand and had a smile to match.

"He would love to, thank you." Elizabeth extracted Rhett from the stroller and held his hand as the woman approached with a leashed dog. Elizabeth pointed at the Canadian license plate.

"You've come a long way for this," Jo said. "Thanks for that."

"We have," she replied. "But it's worth it for us. The circuit gets us out and about. We get cabin bound, if you know what I'm saying.

Crows-feet framed soft brown eyes under the rim of her colorful hat. With tan cheeks in the dead of winter, she looked as though she spent more time outside than in.

"I can understand that," Elizabeth said. "This will be my first winter here, and I've definitely heard stories. I'm Elizabeth, and this is Rhett."

"My mom got us into puzzles to help with the long nights. I'm Keisha, and this is my dog, Buttons. She loves kids. I should know, mine hang all over her."

Rhett ran his fingers along the dog's snout. Buttons nosed him with a snuff.

"I'm Jo. My husband is the course master. And I happen to love puzzles. Your mom's a smart lady."

"Got any you'd like to trade? We have a couple in the van."

"Not with me, but stop by Beans before you leave tomorrow. The owner has plenty to exchange."

Buttons gave Rhett's hand a lick and the boy closed his eyes in delight. "Is he the strong, silent type?"

"Something like that," Elizabeth said. "He loves animals something fierce. Dogs are clearly no exception."

"I may be a bit biased, but I agree. Looks like he'd be okay with a family pet."

A pet dog. One more thing to add to the list of experiences Elizabeth would love to provide her son but could not. Moving out of Casey's house to have a place of her own was step one, but she needed to save up for that. He loved having them there, but Elizabeth had never had a place of her own. She went from her parents' house to married life to her brother's bachelor pad. Somewhere to call her own was something she needed. An accomplishment for her own self-worth.

You'll get there. Keep the faith.

"Thanks for letting us pet Buttons, and good luck in the race." They waved goodbye to their new friends, and Elizabeth wrestled Rhett back into the stroller. He reached out toward the retreating form of Buttons. "She was a sweet dog, wasn't she?"

"Excuse me?" The voice came from the dark and was followed by a woman in a yellow, canvas-fronted jacket who approached with a microphone tucked under one arm. "Would either of you be willing to chat with me about your experience here at the parade? I'm Alma, and I'm making a documentary on the race. I would love to hear from fans."

Jo tipped the corner of her mouth up in a smirk and gestured to Elizabeth. "She's the sport's newest fan. What do you say, my friend?"

Before Elizabeth could splutter out a response, the reporter waved a camera person over. He'd been lingering in the shadows. As the camera guy, a squat man in a baseball cap with long hair pulled into a ponytail, adjusted knobs and flipped switches, the woman straightened her appearance.

First, she fluffed her short, spiky hair, giving Elizabeth a peek of a fleur-de-lis tattoo behind the woman's ear. Dangling, crystal earrings framed her jaw and turquoise lenses made her green irises pop from behind the lenses. The woman had on knee-high gray snow boots and eggplant gloves to complete her rainbow of an outfit. Phone in one hand, microphone in the other, she leaned closer to Elizabeth in the cold.

"Would you please share your name for the camera? Tell us where you're from."

"Oh... sure. I'm Elizabeth Blau. I'm from Seattle."

"Nice to meet you out here on this brisk, celebratory evening." Alma gestured toward the street, and the camera man followed her arm to pan the area. "Can you tell me what it was like to see the dogs today?"

As she asked questions, Alma leaned closer to Elizabeth as though closing the physical space gap would get her closer to the story.

"I've always been a big fan of Christmas lights, and I wanted to share this with my son. It's our first holiday season here."

"Wonderful! Will you be putting up a big tree?"

"Not exactly," Elizabeth said. How could she explain to this stranger that as someone who grew up Jewish, and whose ex-husband was taking her son back to Seattle for Christmas, the holiday season was something she was still figuring out as an adult. "Anyway, we didn't even know about all this. We both love animals and to see the dogs on display was amazing."

"Tell me more about that. What did you think of the drivers? How were the dogs being treated?" Alma's brow pinched together as she waited for Elizabeth's reply.

"We loved all the costumes. The different themes were great." Alma's smile didn't reach her eyes, so Elizabeth continued, "Our friend is one of the racers. He told us all about the dogs, like that they can run over twenty-five miles per hour. Pretty spectacular but not exactly safe on the asphalt of Main Street."

"And what about you, young man?" Alma stooped to address Rhett. "Care to comment on the night?" She tilted the microphone toward his face. Rhett stared at it as though it were an intruder.

They hadn't heard the loaded Black Dogs van inch up until it idled near them. Winton Black had the driver's side window rolled down. "I thought I asked you to leave. These are working people. It's late. Let people go home."

"Yeah. You aren't going to make it to Hollywood with a backcountry video you post on some social media." Bobby Black hung out the passenger window and slapped his hand against the door for emphasis. "Go back to Denver. Go on, now."

Alma put her hands on her hips and faced the brothers. "And I told you I have every right to be at a *public* event." The cameraman shifted the lens to capture the exchange. Alma faced down the duo. "I asked them if they wanted to talk, and they did. Why do you care what other people say? Unless you have something to hide."

"We should go." Jo scooped up Rhett and steered the stroller back toward the parade tent.

Winton gave Alma a dismissive wave and drove off. Alma stared after the van in a refusal to back down. "Bullies."

"Good luck with your documentary." Elizabeth felt pity for the woman. The brothers were right, though. It was late, and she craved a warm bed. "I hope you get your footage."

"Something tells me we will," Alma said, eyes following the Blacks' tail lights. She didn't look back at Elizabeth. "Enjoy your evening."

"Well, that was awkward," Elizabeth said.

"May it be the oddest part of the night," Jo said, and tousled Rhett's hair.

5

THE LAST OF THE trailers backed out of their extended spaces and drove off into the night, crimson taillights trailing their path. Rhett's eyelids drooped as he snuggled into Jo's shoulder.

"How about I walk you to your car? Clint might be a while yet. I don't want to wake the little cowboy," she whispered. When they'd stopped by the tent, Jo's husband was in the process of having his ear talked off by one of the event managers. He'd raised his eyebrows and lifted a hand to acknowledge the trio.

Frost shimmered on the sidewalks. As the night crept forward, the cold came alongside. Elizabeth could see her breath, little puffs against the light of the streetlamp.

"Are you sure? It's only a couple blocks. Who'll walk you back?"

"It'll give me something to do. Keep me warm. If I get back and Clint is still yammering, I'll have an excuse to interrupt. Lynette is the kind of person you love because she is so detail-oriented yet is also the kind of person you could never get off the phone for that exact same reason."

They crossed Main toward Elizabeth's car. She'd snagged a spot on a side street. Her tiny car was easy to fit in spots where trucks didn't have a chance.

By day, the downtown blocks were all hustle and bustle. This evening, as a soft snowfall began, the streets were eerie in their sudden emptiness.

Families had packed their children into cars, tucked blankets around their nodding heads. Exhausted shopkeepers locked front doors, committed to coming back for more tomorrow. The same window displays that were joyful when lit were empty and cold now in the dark.

Elizabeth praised her last-minute splurge on a pair of hand-knitted gloves from a street vendor. The thick clothing kept the cold from reaching her fingertips.

One of Rhett's boots slipped off a foot as his body sagged onto Jo in sleep. Elizabeth stooped to retrieve the shoe. As she crouched near the doorway of the stationary shop, she saw a huddled figure in the doorway.

Boot in hand, she approached.

Tawny-colored hair covered an animal that shivered in the shadows. The creature had tucked itself into a tight circle. Nose under hind leg, the position would stave off some of the bitter cold. Darker brown ears marked the head of a dog bigger than a cocker spaniel but smaller than an Australian shepherd. It appeared to be a mutt, a hodgepodge of genetics. Its eyes closed against the elements, it had not stirred on their approach. Elizabeth struggled to understand how anyone or anything could sleep in the frigid elements.

Jo stopped behind Elizabeth, her gaze following her friend's attention. She took the boot from Elizabeth's hand to wedge it back on Rhett's foot. "Oh, the poor thing. We can call someone. I know a vet in town. Just a sec." She handed Rhett over to Elizabeth before rummaging in her purse for her phone.

Elizabeth tucked Rhett onto one hip. Jostled awake, her son's sleepy lashes blinked open against his cheeks. When he saw what had interrupted his slumber, he reached out toward the sleeping bundle with one little hand. "Dog."

At the sound of his voice, the women froze.

6

T HE NEXT FEW MINUTES were a blur as Jo hovered around the animal making phone calls. She'd whipped off the flannel underneath her jacket and laid it over the dog. With a tender touch, she felt for a pulse, checked her nose, and tried to assess for injuries without moving the creature. Clint arrived a few minutes later, his presence demanded, and joined in the assessment.

Elizabeth could only stand in silent shock as the two other adults buzzed around her with plans. She was a statue around which the others carried on as though their lives, her life, had not been rocked to its core.

Ten minutes later, with the help of the vet, the Wolfs placed the dog on a makeshift stretcher. The animal let out a soft, plaintive whine when it was moved but otherwise was quiet. One leg lay at an awkward angle.

Their conversation was a buzz in Elizabeth's subconscious as her mind circled again and again. Her son had said his first word.

Jo and Clint each took one end of the stretcher to load it into the vet's truck. Before they could step forward, Elizabeth interrupted. "Wait! Let me take him."

"Are you sure?" Jo looked at Elizabeth as though she'd forgotten her friend was there.

"We've got a snug laundry room," Clint said. "And golden retrievers get along with everyone."

The vet addressed the group. "I gave her a sedative for the ride, but I should follow you. Help settle her in. Just let me know where."

Her.

Elizabeth knew there was no way she would willingly let the inspiration for her son's first word out of her sight.

"I'm sure."

After the vet had come and gone, Jo and Elizabeth watched the dog sleep from the bar stools that fronted Casey's kitchen island. They'd fashioned a makeshift bed from an old wrestling mat and barn blankets Casey had in storage.

The vet had wrapped the leg to stabilize it. He'd secured a promise from Elizabeth to bring the dog in the next morning for x-rays and to scan for a microchip.

The dog was asleep, the soft rise and fall of its belly a rhythm of hope. A single snore escaped her snout, but otherwise, the animal was quiet, deep in dreamland.

Each woman clutched a cup of tea in her hands. Jo had grown the chamomile and peppermint herself. She'd gifted sachets of the garden harvest to Elizabeth, who savored the soothing blend. The warm ceramic was a comfort.

"They say being within proximity of an animal lowers your blood pressure," Elizabeth said.

"I believe it. I don't think I would've made it through my teenage years without our border collie. I cried into his coat many a night."

"Thanks for calling the vet. I wouldn't have known what to do."

"What good are favors owed if you never call them in? Tim owes me for more than one referral. He normally handles big animals, loves to land a fancy equine client, and Clint meets lots of those."

"Those are Casey's clients, too." When he wasn't tending to his goats and the cheese business, Casey redesigned the interiors of Big Horn mansions.

Jo pushed back her barstool and walked the mug to the sink. "I'll get out of your hair. You sure you're going to be okay tonight?"

"I can manage until the morning. Casey will be back early. Said he'd help me bring her in. That will go easier if she swallows the pill the vet left, but I'm hoping a hunk of Casey's cheddar will help. Either way, we'll get her there."

Jo shrugged into her coat and stepped to the door. One hand on the threshold, she paused. "Would you like to talk about what happened?"

Elizabeth had not been certain, until this moment, that anyone else had heard Rhett speak. She'd wondered if it was a figment of her imagination, wishful thinking that manifested in a tense moment.

"I...don't know."

"No worries," Jo said. "We're here if you need us. For anything. A phone call away."

Elizabeth nodded. Jo reached down to give the dog a soft pat.

"I wish I knew her name," Elizabeth said. *So I can thank her.*

"Here's hoping there's a microchip to help us out," Jo said. "I can't think why anyone would let such a sweet girl out like this, so vulnerable. Goodnight."

Elizabeth had the same question. Was it a matter of cruelty or a dog who'd escaped the trailer and was not found? What if the owners were halfway back to Minnesota, not to return until the race on New Year's? She didn't want to leave the dog in case she woke in the night. Instead of heading down the hall to the room she shared with Rhett, she piled a few of Casey's pillows into a makeshift headrest, tucked a throw blanket around herself, and searched the television offerings for a movie.

In the morning, there would be answers.

7

LEMON YELLOW LIGHT STREAKED with blue spread across the great room of Casey's house. Elizabeth blinked herself awake. A patch of drool stood out on the dusty pink surface of a square pillow. She stretched and yawned.

The dog watched Elizabeth. Big brown eyes, deep in a wide face. Elizabeth reached for the hoodie she'd draped across the back of the couch.

"Let's see if you need a break outside."

Before she could offer support, the animal attempted to stand. There was a wince as she put weight on the injured leg.

"Easy girl, let me help you." Elizabeth approached her with care. She held out the back of her hand to be sniffed. The dog gave her a soft lick of consent.

With one arm around each side of the dog's big chest, Elizabeth lifted her out of the bed and carried her to the door. She must've weighed sixty pounds, twice the heft of Rhett. Too late, she realized opening the door would be difficult with a dog in her arms. Elizabeth lifted one foot, balanced on the other, and kicked at the door handle.

The door popped open to reveal Casey, backpack slung over one shoulder, hand held out, about to put his key in the lock. "I have so many questions."

"It's a long story. Can it wait until after I take her outside for a minute?"

"I've got the door." He held it open while she maneuvered out, careful with the dog's legs.

"Put on a fresh pot, please," Elizabeth said. "We're going to need one."

She walked the dog out to a patch of grass and set her down. The morning was crisp. A single crow cawed out from a telephone pole.

Nick, Elizabeth's ex-husband, had never wanted a dog. He'd claimed their townhouse was much too small and Rhett was much too fragile to have an animal bustling about underfoot. Like many disappointments in their marriage, Elizabeth had swept the idea to the back of her mind where she cataloged her lost hopes.

Warm dog back in her arms, she tapped at the door with the toe of her shoe. Casey opened it, and the aroma of Arabica beans filled her nostrils.

"This should be interesting," he said. "I poured you a mug."

8

"I 'VE GOT HALF A dozen turkeys to sort out, and it is the absolute wrong time of year to have that problem."

A faint gobble could be heard behind the voice coming through the speaker. Elizabeth could picture Corbin, the manager of a local animal rescue agency, on his small ranch spread as he contemplated his newest, feathered residents.

"Live ones, right?"

"You nailed it. A sweet retiree from near Parkman rescued them over the last couple of years in a bid to convince her neighbors to go vegetarian. Now I've got to find honest homes for all of them. Worst time of year for it, though."

"Good luck with that," Elizabeth said.

She'd called Corbin, the owner of a local no-kill rescue agency. With a limited operating budget and a staff of one, Corbin leveraged his network of animal lovers to rescue as many cases as he could. Jo had met Corbin when she adopted Bessie and Buck that summer.

A mountain man with wolfish teeth, a permanent shadow of a beard, and a shock of chestnut hair, Corbin could be a model from an outdoor clothing catalog.

"At any rate, that's my current problem," he said. "What can I do for you?"

Elizabeth filled him in on the details of finding the dog. She told him what the vet said and the care she's delivered since bringing her home.

"No collar?"

"Nothing."

"And you found her at a time when there had just been dozens of dogs in the downtown area, so she could belong to any number of out-of-town people, let alone locals."

"That's why I'm hoping you'll swing by. Give me some guidance."

"In a slightly more ideal situation, I would be able to pick her up right away. Get her to a foster spot. We have lots of vets we work with on the regular, pro bono. They'd figure out her injuries. Then we could start putting out notices. Send them to the drivers who were here last night."

Elizabeth thought about her meager savings. She couldn't do this on her own. "So what about a less than ideal situation?"

"Give me a day. I'll try to get a hold of someone to pick her up, and we can take it from there. A lot of people just head to the pound. When it comes to injured animals, they don't have as many options as I do."

"She's really sweet. I hope we can find her owner." Elizabeth knew she didn't mean that last sentence. The more she talked about their house guest leaving, the less she wanted to help it happen.

"A dog that awesome has to have someone looking for her."

9

"WHEN I LEFT, CASEY was brushing her with one of the combs from the barn. He's smitten," Elizabeth said.

Jo chuckled. "Sounds about right. I've yet to meet an animal that man couldn't charm. Good thing he isn't into alligators or anything wild."

"Don't give him any ideas. Rhett would want one in the bathtub."

Elizabeth leaned over the stall door to reach a tentative hand toward Bessie. On cue, the donkey flattened her ears in an invitation for a scratch. She'd mellowed in the months since coming to live with Jo and Clint.

"A neighbor back home had a pack of Sicilian donkeys. Sweet creatures and full of personality, just like Bessie. She likes you," Jo said.

"And I like her. And you," Elizabeth said to Buck. The huge goat watched her from the corner of his stall with horizontal pupils. Bessie and Buck were a package deal. Buck was protective of his donkey friend. His ornery personality, distrustful of strangers, had saved Jo's life a few months before.

"They really do make great pets," Jo said. "I have Casey to thank for the platform idea." Jo had constructed a series of shelves for Buck to climb from Bessie's stall up and over into his own stall and back whenever he liked. "How's the pup?"

Elizabeth had come over to update Jo. The latter was in the barn, mucking out stalls. Elizabeth picked up a rake to collect stray strands littered across the planked floor.

"A couple of times, she tried to get up and follow me around the house. I didn't want her hurting herself, so I put the dog bed in Rhett's wagon and dragged her around with me while I folded the laundry and ran through Casey's books. It was like she didn't want to let me out of her sight."

"A working dog, a running dog. Makes sense."

Elizabeth remembered how sled after sled of dogs paraded down the street. While the majority were huskies, that wasn't true for all of them. Her dog could have been a member of a team.

Clint knocked on the barn door and entered. He was in uniform, badge at his chest, gun on his belt. His granite eyes were weary. "Hey, honey. Liz. Let me get changed, and I'll help."

"'Bout time. Typical of you to show up as I'm finishing up with choring," Jo teased. Her husband dropped a kiss on her lips.

"Did the dog get scanned?"

"The software kept resetting, so I have to go back on Tuesday," Elizabeth said.

Clint pressed his lips together and nodded. "We need confirmation, but I think Ryland found the owner."

"That's wonderful news," Jo said. She paused her shoveling to wipe at her sweaty brow with the back of one hand.

Elizabeth felt her heart sink into a soft place, low in her gut. On the one hand, she was happy the owner could be reunited with their pet. On the other, the dog had filled a space in the Blau home Elizabeth hadn't known was empty. She didn't want to let that go.

"Only one problem," Clint said. He took off his hat and scratched at his forehead.

"Problem?"

"The man's dead."

10

"WE'RE GOING TO NEED a little more detail, Sheriff." Jo said. The pragmatic one, she kept a legal pad and pen on a clipboard in the barn. She snagged it down from a nail on the wall and readied herself. There wasn't anything she couldn't notate.

Clint had disappeared into the house for a few minutes and returned in barn clothes, rugged pants, long-sleeved shirt, and a fleece vest. He picked up a shovel and went to work while he talked.

"I thought I recognized the type of dog from the parade. I scrolled through Ryland's pictures. Your girl is a ringer for one of the dogs in the pack owned by Black Dogs."

Elizabeth peeled off a slab of barley straw and heaved it into Bessie's feed box. "They only breed one type?"

"No, they diversify. It's sort of their specialty. Winton is the operations side of the business, and Bobby is the driver. Teamwork seems to drive their brand, thick as thieves they've been since they were kids," Jo said. "Their father was the sweetest of men. Mother, on the other hand, was something else. She would regularly turn the kids out and lock the doors for the day, leaving the brothers to fend for themselves."

"My uncle had to chase them out of the garden," Clint said. "Took him a few years to realize they weren't stealing extras, just trying to stay fed."

Elizabeth could relate. The cupboards of the Blau house hadn't been bare, but it had been unusual for them to contain a meal. Bread but no lunch meat. Cereal but no milk. "That's a hard way to grow up."

"'Tis. I went by the kennels today. No one around but one of the hands. Said they hadn't seen either brother since last night. On my way back down, I got a call from dispatch. Staff member found their boss at the bottom of a cliff, one of those rock climber crags."

Jo scratched the pen against the paper, then paused. "At the bottom? Like he fell?"

"Don't know for sure. Yet. Ryland is out there with the state's team trying to figure that out. The employee called it in, said she'd noticed a couple of the dogs were missing. She pulled up their tags. Tracked the signals to the cliff face. One was down at the bottom, circling Winton's body while the others howled nearby."

Elizabeth pictured the gruesome scene. Dogs mourning the loss of their alpha. The cold, the cliffside. A once warm and living human, cold and still on the rocks.

"Were they able to round up the dogs?" She couldn't bear to think of dogs freezing outside as they mourned the loss of their pack.

"All but one. Winton's favorite big old sled dog refused to leave his side. Named Brutus. He growled when we approached. Had to wait for Corbin to come and help."

"Poor thing," Jo said. "He was probably scared."

Clint leaned against the barn wall on one shoulder and crossed his arms over his chest, the handle of the rake under his armpit. Jo reached over to brush a flake of hay off his jacket.

"Ryland almost lost his nerve. Brutus had blood around his mouth. We worried about rabies and all that, so we called Corbin."

Elizabeth shuddered. "You don't think—"

"Nah. We'll have to wait a bit for the coroner report, but it didn't look like Winton was bleeding other than...well."

"I met Brutus before," Jo said. "Scruffy gentle giant. Feather-soft fur. Winton loved him."

"Where's the dog now?" Elizabeth couldn't help her curiosity. When she'd opened her heart to the rescue dog, there was no closing the door.

"Corbin has him. It was a fight to keep him out of the county facility. We'll see how long it lasts."

11

B ACK HOME, ELIZABETH SAT with the dog in her lap and stroked her soft ears.

"That's quite the dramatic ending," Casey said.

"Clint is sure she belongs to them." Elizabeth continued to pat the dog. The animal in question lolled in Elizabeth's lap, content. "Apparently, they raise fancy sled dogs. Sell them all over the U.S. and Canada."

"So, what do you do now?" Casey scooped a ladle full of cooled stew into a dog dish. He'd insisted on making the mixture himself after a morning searching for homemade dog food recipes.

"I have to take her back for another scan. Get a chip confirmed. That's step one."

Casey portioned the rest of the stew into storage containers. He snapped a matching yellow lid to the top of each.

Rhett wandered out from his room to plant himself in the dog bed. He hung his little legs over the edge of the cardboard box, a plastic bowl of dry cereal in his lap while he watched cartoons.

"Still in pjs, I see. Come on, let's get dressed." She held out her arms to Rhett.

"Oh, hey," Casey called after her. "Nick called me looking for you. Said you haven't called him back."

Elizabeth sighed and scooted Rhett into the bedroom. Once she had her son dressed in a pair of jeans and a Wyo sweatshirt, she returned Nick's call. "How's the weather over there? Full-on rainy season yet?"

"Cut the crap. I deserve an update."

"Studies show people handle big news better when it's prefaced with small talk." Elizabeth was buying time with distraction. She twirled a lock of hair around one finger. There didn't seem to be a way to tell Nick she had nothing new to say. She wanted to have good news, amazing news, but there wasn't more.

"Is he talking right now? Put him on. I want to hear. You know what? I'll just drive over there."

"Wait. Hold on. He's only said it twice, Nick," she said. "There's nothing new to share. Yet."

"Are you sure he said dog? Not Dad?"

Elizabeth pressed her lips together. The strife of the last few months poured back onto her shoulders. After an attempt at Nick's life, there'd been a cooling of their animosity. Like it or not, they were inextricably linked through the life of the little boy they both loved so much.

"He said dog because we found one. We found her, and she was injured, and that's a long story. We're trying to find the owner, but I wanted to call you and let you know."

"This is huge. I'm gonna call my mom."

"Wait." Words spilled out before she could stop herself from letting them loose. "I think you were right about contacting a specialist."

12

B AGS CLUTCHED IN EACH hand, Elizabeth shuffled through the doorway and set the load on the counter. The house was quiet.

"Hello?" She tucked the milk and eggs in the fridge and called again. "Casey?"

Elizabeth tamped down the kernel of fear that bloomed in her stomach. Silent houses were bad news in her book. The rest of the groceries could wait. She would find her family first.

Casey's house was modest in size, impeccable in design, his architecture degree on full display in the build. Vaulted ceilings and skylights gave it a spacious air. Clean lines, white surfaces, and brushed stainless steel covered his canvas. A dozen throw pillows, a trunk of rodeo memorabilia, and a growing gallery of pictures of his nephew gave a little personality. He specialized in magazine-quality appearances and had an extensive waitlist for his services.

The open concept living areas led to a short hallway of bedrooms that ended with a door to the backyard. She headed outside to find her family.

Elizabeth jogged across the dusty ground and made for the barn. She'd neglected to throw on a jacket and only a flannel protected her from the brisk December chill. She shivered at the touch of the smooth metal of the barn door handle, frigid in her hands. With a quick shove, she wedged her way inside the building and into some relative warmth.

The scent of hay mixed with animal bodies filled her nostrils. The first stall housed Casey's horse. Her nose in a feed bag, the bay roan munched at its contents.

In a corner of the structure sat a couple opened boxes, the few new pieces of brewing equipment she'd been able to afford on her first few months of salary. A milk crate held some hosing and thermometers. The fermenter was still in its wrapping, and a couple of glass carboys waited, empty. Brewing was a temperature-sensitive activity, and while Casey gave a green light to brewing indoors, Elizabeth needed a few more pieces of equipment before she would dust off her old skill set.

Soft murmurings came from deeper within the barn. She followed the sound.

Her brother had carried the dog and little boy, box and all, out to the barn on a pallet jack. Parked near the goat enclosure, dog and boy watched as Casey fed the herd.

Elizabeth paused in place for a moment to drink in the vignette. As Rhett watched his uncle minister to the goats, his soft, pink lips moved, as though narrating the process for the dog. To her credit, their new canine friend watched the goats as though she hung onto his every word.

"Here you are. Looks like feeding time," said Elizabeth.

"Didn't make sense to leave them inside," Casey said.

Elizabeth joined them. She leaned over the railing, resting her forearms against the bar. She wanted to take a picture, to capture what had seemed so out of reach only months before, but no photo could do this moment justice.

She had a family. A small, tight, family. The love in the room was almost more than she could bear.

"The three of you are peas in a pod. Have room for one more?"

<hr/>

Later, after Rhett was asleep, Casey joined her on the couch. They'd found an old western, a cowboy crossing the screen in black and white, nothing but his horse and the scenery for miles.

"I keep thinking I'd like to get some chickens—for the eggs—but Jo scared me off with her horror story about a badger inside the coop. I'd get some tomorrow if I had a dog around."

"You'd have the most stylish chicken coop in a tri-county area."

"You're darn right I would," Casey said. He held his wine glass up in a mock toast. But, also, I'm guessing you and Rhett might move out into your own place someday. This house will be mighty empty with just me bumping about inside. Having a built-in best friend would go a long way."

"It's definitely not your worst idea." Casey threw a pillow at Elizabeth and she stood to avoid its path. "Back in a minute. I think I need to make a phone call."

Elizabeth sat on her navy comforter and crossed one leg over the other while the phone rang, a soft chirrup through the speaker.

"Burro Buddies," answered the sleepy voice.

"It's me, Liz Blau. Sorry to wake you."

"Don't tell me you found a wayward elephant. Or a vicious crocodile?"

Elizabeth sank into the sound of his husky voice. She wanted to be someone he favored. Someone he trusted. "Nothing like. Casey and I were just talking. Well, we were wondering...I was wondering...if we can foster the dog. You know, until whatever is happening with her ownership sorts out."

"Oh. Well. There's some paperwork," he said. "If you're sure, we can make this happen."

"Great," she said to the receiver and heaved a sigh of relief. The dog could be theirs, at least for now. "Thank you."

"Don't thank me yet," Corbin said. "The ink's hardly dry."

13

O N Monday morning, Casey gave Jo a break and kept Rhett with him. "Someone has to keep an eye on the dog. Besides, I get to become a foster dad today. We can celebrate when you get home."

Elizabeth brewed a pot of coffee and assembled a stack of sandwiches for the household. A morsel of gouda hit the tile and bounced a few inches. The dog sniffed at the hunk, then snapped it up. After that, she followed Elizabeth's every move, shuffling her wounded leg across the floor.

Stirrings from the bedrooms signaled that her family was awake. She plated her breakfast of veggie hash and poured a steaming cup of coffee into an oversized mug Casey had brought back from Yellowstone. She would need the extra caffeine this week.

As Elizabeth perched on the bar stool, digging into breakfast, she stroked the dog's belly with the big toe of one foot. The animal had tucked herself under the stool, whether in protection or to lay claim to the occasional egg bit that would hit the ground, Elizabeth didn't know. Breakfast finished, she offered the crust from her toast. The dog gobbled it up with joy.

"Don't get too used to that," Elizabeth said. "Casey said dogs should not eat people food. He's got fancier things planned for your meals than he does for ours, and that's saying something."

The dog followed Elizabeth into the tiny laundry room where she pulled a blouse from the dryer. She shook it free of wrinkles, then turned around and almost tripped over the knee-high obstacle whose tail gave an affirmative wag.

"I wish I knew your name," Elizabeth said.

The dog pressed her nose against Elizabeth's leg and thumped her tail against the tile floor. Her big brown eyes were deep pools, devoted. Elizabeth scratched between the dog's ears, and the dog's tail wagged in delight.

"Maybe I'll call you Shadow for now. You are good at sticking with a person. Loyal. I hope your real name isn't something like Trixie or Duchess."

The dog tilted her head, listening to Elizabeth talk. One leg stretched out from the others as she rested her haunches on the floor. The caramel-colored fur at her shoulders twitched, as though she anticipated Elizabeth's next move. "I don't think I'm interesting enough to deserve a groupie, pup."

Clint was right. A sled dog would need to be this attentive. Ready to shift into action at a moment's notice.

Elizabeth carried the full basket out to the living room where Casey had molded himself into the couch, a game on the screen.

"I see what you've been saying," Elizabeth said. "Sticks to me like glue."

"She assumes you're worth the attention. I know better."

Elizabeth wadded up Casey's washed sweatshirt and threw it at his head.

"Easy there. It was just a joke."

"You're right. I'm just hoping whomever owns her, deserves her."

14

E LIZABETH'S LUNCH BAG WAS wedged between the pre-packaged salads, bottles of dressing, diet soda, and leftover birthday cupcakes that crowded the work room fridge.

"Good Thanksgiving?"

Startled, Elizabeth hit her head on the upper door to the freezer. She winced from the pain and backed out, one hand pressing the tender spot.

Maggie, a short, squat toad of a woman, filled the doorway. She was the bus driver, lunch lady, and de facto maintenance person for the school. Her mother had been a teacher but died young from a one-two punch of emphysema and COPD.

"We did. Kept it small. You?"

"Sometimes that's just the ticket," Maggie said. She plopped herself in a chair at the small Formica table and withdrew a paper from under her arm. A glance at the clock told Liz the woman had another quarter hour before she would head out to pick up the kids.

"We found a lost dog," Elizabeth said.

"Were you able to find the owners? We lost our Rocket for a whole twenty-four hours once. Turned out my Hank left her in the backseat of the car when he brought the groceries in. Sweet man but has the brains of a box of rocks some days. She wasn't too bad off, but the backseat was a mess."

"My brother is taking her in to get scanned for a chip. Maybe we'll find the owners. Sheriff told me she's probably a sled dog."

Maggie flipped through a few pages, then tossed the paper on the table. "They've got lots of stamina, to be sure. Keep them busy, or they'll find their own occupation, if you know what I mean."

Elizabeth wasn't sure she did. "Did you grow up with them?"

Maggie leaned back in the rickety chair and interlaced her fingers over her ample chest. "No, but I've seen the race a time or two. There's something amazing about that kind of endurance. A sled dog crew is like a family. They all look out for each other. Even move together. Like a storm cloud across the prairie. Beautiful to see."

Elizabeth slipped out of her coat and hung it on a peg. "I've been thinking I might go see the race."

Maggie tapped an article in a news column. Winton's face smiled up from a photo. "Speaking of sled dogs, did you see this?" She rested a stubby, plum-painted fingernail on the paper. "A shame. I grew up with Winton. Was the type to mow everyone's lawns in the summer for nothing but a scout badge. Heard they found him alone with only old Brutus for company. He and Bobby built themselves a pretty nice spread up there. Didn't save his marriage, but they say money can't buy that kind of stuff."

"It sure doesn't."

She pushed the paper in Elizabeth's direction. LO-CAL BREEDER DEAD, INVESTIGATION ONGOING was scrawled above the article. "I should go and warm up the bus. Enjoy a little peace in silence while you can. The littles are often wound up after the holiday weekend."

Elizabeth scanned the short story. Black had been found dead on his ranch, his loyal dog by his side. The brief left out any question of how the tragedy happened. The reporter noted that Winton and his brother were successful local business owners and that his contributions to the community would be missed.

Across the front page was an article dedicated to the weekend's dog sled parade. The main picture was of Santa, Gary's eyes crinkled beneath the costume. A smaller set of photos depicted Bobby Black at the helm of his sled, his team focused on the road ahead. In another, the women dressed in purple smiled at the camera, their arms around each other.

The paper stretched out in front of her, Elizabeth took another look at the photo of Bobby, his team small in the photo. The gray, black, and white dogs looked nothing like the brown at Elizabeth's house. As though made from cookie cutters, each animal in front of Bobby was a match for the next. Like canine robots, they trotted in line.

In each photo, along the sidewalk, townsfolk stood shoulder to shoulder watching the sleds go by. Many held thermoses between gloved hands. Others were turned toward the person next to them, mouths open in mid commentary.

One person stood out among the rest. It took Elizabeth a moment to recognize the rectangular box in front of one face as a camera. Next to the camera was a woman who clutched a microphone in her hand, her eyes on Bobby Black. It was Alma, the documentary maker.

A self-proclaimed dog lover, the glare in her expression was nothing short of ominous.

15

E LIZABETH HAD TWO PHONE calls to make and exactly twelve minutes in which to make them.

A half hour for lunch had to include a trip to the bathroom, a rushed inhalation of her sandwich, and the interruption of her coworker droning on about her sister's wedding.

The first call went straight to Casey's voicemail. This was typical. She left a voicemail that asked for an update text.

The next order of business required a specific sticky note she'd squirreled away in her purse.

"Dr. Reynolds' office."

Elizabeth heard the buzz of office activity through the phone speaker. Murmurs of adults in the background made for a continuous hum punctuated by the occasional shriek of a toddler.

"Hi, I...uh. I'm new to the area, and my son just started talking... well, kind of. He just said his first word and I—"

"Wonderful. That is such a fun milestone to reach. Well, not for my sister-in-law. She has five kids and said once they started talking none of them would stop, and there she is in the middle of all that noise. Make sure you take note of the date and bring it in to his next appointment. Would that be the nine-month or the twelve-month? I can add a note to his chart."

"Thank you, but I don't have an appointment yet. Like I said, we're new here."

"Oh yes, silly me. Not a problem. We'll get you sorted in two shakes. Let's start with his name and date of birth please."

Elizabeth spelled Rhett's name while the keyboard clacked on the other end of the line. When she gave his birthday, the sound stopped.

"Could you please repeat that? I don't think I got the numbers correct."

Elizabeth sighed. *You did.* As parental guilt flooded her veins, Elizabeth repeated the date with a pause between each agonizing number so she would not have to say it again.

A beat of silence from the receptionist, then, "I see. One moment while I check in with patient services about our availability. Please hold."

While she waited, a call came through from her brother. Elizabeth would give almost anything to hang up on her current conversation and lose herself in the caretaking of their houseguest. Having it pointed out, again and again, how your child is different was excruciating. She wondered if all parents had this experience or if it was reserved for a small club.

The voice returned to the line. "Ma'am? We can absolutely get you established here for regular checkups. In the meantime, the doctor has a couple of names for you. Specialists."

Elizabeth's cheeks flushed hot, and a twitch went up her spine. "But she hasn't met my son. How could she already recommend a specialist?" Her voice snapped, alongside her patience.

"Let's get you scheduled, so you can discuss this with her. It's just that our next available appointment is a month from now, and she didn't know how long you would want to wait."

Elizabeth gritted her teeth. "When exactly is the next opening?"

With five minutes before she had to summon her energy for a read-aloud with a passel of recess-pumped kindergartners, Elizabeth collapsed into a chair, spent. The receptionist was just doing her job, relaying what she'd been told. In those jobs, one had to walk a delicate line of treating a customer as though they know what they are doing and at the same time, making it clear they do not.

Elizabeth beat herself up enough as a mother. She certainly didn't need more blows from a stranger she would meet on January 11th at two o'clock.

Rita, the lower grades teacher, popped through the door, a small cooler in hand. As the school didn't have enough students for full grade classrooms, staff rotated duties. Rita would enjoy her lunch while Elizabeth read to the students.

"Hey, hun. Doing okay?" Rita wore a sunset-striped shirt that complemented the auburn streaks in her shoulder-length hair. With practiced speed, the woman unwrapped a pita stuffed with veggies from its beeswax-coated wrapping. Elizabeth watched as Rita tipped back in her chair to open the fridge and extract a mason jar from its confines. The liquid inside was yellowish and fizzy. "Kombucha," she said to Elizabeth. "I started making it myself. It's just so expensive to buy."

"Looks...refreshing."

A few white globules from the SCOBY floated on the liquid. She'd gone through a phase of making it herself as well, the giant jar resting on a high shelf in the pantry. Nick never liked it, though. Said it was too sour. After six months, she rehomed her set-up. Maybe she could start it up again. "We...I used to make it, too. Always wanted to add flavor to mine but never got it right. Had a few countertop explosions."

Rita laughed, a bird-like sound. "I think it's like anything in life, you just do your best and be okay with the messy results."

First one tear and then three more hit Elizabeth's cheeks. She sniffed, then wiped at her eyes with the sleeve of her shirt. Rita watched, concern written in the lines on her forehead as Elizabeth took in a chestful of air and then let it out, slow and measured. Rita, an experienced kindergarten teacher who'd seen many tears in her career, was patient.

"I'm sorry. I'm not usually like this." This was only her third month at a school where most of the staff had known each other for decades. What impression would this make? She'd already been moved here because of violence at her own school. Elizabeth saw the whispers, felt the curious stares at her back when she'd arrived. Still, this was her work, for now, and she was human. A crushed human. "It's... my son. I don't know if you have kids, but you work with kids, and I don't know, I just feel like with my own son, I never quite know what I'm doing. Like I'm flailing in the dark sometimes. Like if anything good happens, it was dumb luck I can't replicate."

Rita put her hand on Elizabeth's elbow. The gentle reassurance made tears well again.

"Do any of us ever *really* know what we're doing in the grand scheme of things? I'm up to my ears in college debt. I can't change a tire. I only date commitment-phobes with bad hygiene. We just have to keep putting one foot in front of the other until we get to the feeling of control again. That's all we can do. But control is an illusion, isn't it? Doesn't mean we can't be our own best cheerleaders through it all. Life is too short to put energy into being your own worst enemy."

Rita's words infused Elizabeth's afternoon like a soft snowfall. When panic threatened to well up in her stomach, she forced herself to remember the woman's careful advice.

By the end of the day, as she waved to Maggie while the bus left the tiny parking lot, Elizabeth's mood had lifted.

A buzzing in her pocket alerted her to a call from Casey.

"When will you be home? The dog got out."

16

"**W**HAT DO YOU MEAN?" Her voice was steel. Powered by reflex, she ran to grab her things. "Tell me what happened."

She swapped the phone from one ear to the other hand and clutched it between chin and shoulder as she unlocked her car. With a toss of her shoulder, her bag plopped onto the passenger seat. The engine gave a small, rumbled protest. *Not now*, she told it, and shifted into gear.

"Vet check went fine," Casey said. "He reset the leg. Gave me some directions for PT. Clint was here for the scan, but then he took off."

"Get to the part where the dog is gone." Elizabeth drove without seeing, praying the miles would pass faster.

"I walked Doc out to the barn so he could check on some of the nannies. Brought the dog out with me, but when we turned back, she was gone. He's out there calling for her. I think Rhett's starting to wonder where she is. I don't even know what name to yell, Liz."

The ache in his voice went straight to her heart. Casey Blau wasn't the emotional type. His version of managing feelings involved watching wrestling tournaments and rodeos from his youth, a cold beer in hand. His first inclination, like hers, was escape. It surprised her now, to hear the tremble in his voice, the unsteadiness.

"Be there soon. Keep Rhett distracted."

Miles flew by as Elizabeth's mind raced alongside. Her mind whipped through a dozen scenarios in which her little shadow was injured, lost, and again abandoned to fate. No creature should feel that way, let alone twice.

Casey's ranch was small compared to the expensive cattle operations in the area, but he still had significant acreage. A few tall trees scattered around his yard, and the brush was low and sparse. This time of year, the dog should be easy to see if she wandered off, but she could've gone in any number of directions.

A man stood at the edge of the driveway, binoculars glued to his face.

Elizabeth braked the car into the gravel and hopped out. "Any sign of Shadow? I mean, the dog."

"Not yet. I don't understand. She was right there with us."

Inside, Casey held a squirmy toddler in his arms. Both uncle and nephew gave Elizabeth a look of sheer relief.

"Here," she said, and reached out for her son. "I'll take him. You help with the search."

Casey dashed out the door. Rhett fussed in her arms. He twisted his head from side to side as he looked for his furry friend. "How about a snack? Maybe that will give us something to do while we wait. What do you say?"

Elizabeth held her son in one arm and built peanut butter graham cracker sandwiches with the other. More peanut butter ended up on the counter than on the crackers. She set the three successful attempts on a plate before handing them over to Rhett. She saved the ugliest one for herself. Rhett dug in as Elizabeth nibbled.

On the countertop in front of her lay a few pieces of paper. Blue ink scrawled across several, and she scanned their contents while she chewed.

The first few were from Burro Buddies and outlined the expectations of fostering an animal. The other two were from the vet. One detailed directions for helping the pup heal from her injury: keep the wrapping as clean as possible and monitor activity. The last sheet listed details from the visit, including the dog's general health, description of the injury, and the results of her microchip scan. Elizabeth's breath caught in her throat when she read that last note.

Casey burst in the front door. Both mother and son swiveled to the sound.

"We found her! Dan is checking her over again." Casey braced himself on the counter as his breath heaved. "Hang on. My heart wants to punch right through my chest."

"Where was she?"

"Stuck in the old chicken coop. Dan heard a faint whining and went over to check."

Elizabeth's pulse slowed, and she pressed her hands on her cheeks. "Okay. Can I just say how much I freaked out when you called me?"

"You and me, both. Looks like I'll be working on that penthouse coop sooner than I planned. At this point, the old one's a hazard."

The door opened again, and the man she'd seen in the driveway when she arrived, an older man wearing overalls and an I'd Rather Be Fishing hat, ushered the wayward dog inside. Rhett's face lit up as the dog ambled toward his chair and licked at the boy's toes.

"Right as rain," the vet said. "Well, as right as you can be with a fracture. She'll be okay though. Strong dog. I did wonder, though, and Casey couldn't tell me. Any idea how it happened?"

Around the dog's leg was a neat wrapping that circled it like a maypole. "She was injured when we found her. I wish we knew more."

"Hard to be sure without X-rays, but I'd swear she has other tender spots. And when I took out the scanner and again with my tablet when I took a picture, she winced. Usually, dogs only do that if they think they're about to get hit. Makes me wonder about her home life."

"I'll tell Corbin what you found," Casey said.

"Thank you, again," Elizabeth said. "Pretty sure you've gone above and beyond the call of duty today."

"Casey is one of my favorite customers, and I'm happy to help. Just glad we found her," Dan said. "Call me if anything changes. She should be healed up and running in a matter of weeks."

Casey walked the man to the door. When he turned back to face his sister, she held one of the papers out toward him.

"Tell me you saw this."

17

*W*INTON *B*LACK.

Written in the owner spot on the printed page. Elizabeth could still see it when she closed her eyes.

What this meant for her, for all of them, she didn't know.

In the parking lot of Sheridan Feed, she eased her hatchback into a space between two extra-tall, extra-wide trucks and dialed a now familiar number.

"Hey Liz," Corbin said. "Is this about Leia?"

"Leia?" A bubble of familiarity tried to surface in her brain. She'd been so fixated on the discovery, all the other information was fuzzy in the background.

"The dog. Clint told me the scan came up with an owner. I figured you knew." A sudden eruption of barking nearby prompted Corbin to interrupt their call. "One sec, there's someone at the door. "

Leia. Of course her name would come up in addition to the owner's information. She should have read the paper more closely, digested its entirety.

Corbin returned to the phone a minute later. "Sorry about that. Best doorbell I can have is a dog. A little too effective sometimes. I've been waiting on these pills, though. I've got a llama with some serious arthritis."

"A llama?"

"Day in the life. Speaking of foster animals, how is Leia?"

While she didn't want to lie to Corbin, she didn't want to alarm him either. Telling him they lost the dog within the first day wouldn't do much for their reputation as foster parents.

She waffled between telling him and not. Did he need to know? "When I left just now, she was inside by the fire, snoring away."

"Living the good life, then?" He chuckled, and Elizabeth's nerves began to ease.

She picked out a loose flap in the upholstery of her driver seat. "I came into town to get some more supplies and wondered how much I should buy. You know, since we know the owner now." A quick check of her bank account revealed a need to keep things tight if there would be any presents in the Blau household.

"Oh. Of course. I forgot this is your first foster."

A look of pity edged his voice, and she didn't want that between them. "I just wanted to check in and see when we might know something."

"As sad as it is to share, this isn't the first situation I've experienced where the owner has died and an animal is involved. Makes things complicated. I'm always telling people they need to leave plans for their pets in their will. Hardly anyone listens, though. Except the parrot owners. Maybe that's more of a thing when your chosen pet is likely to outlive you."

Corbin's voice soothed her nerves, and she wished he were there in person. She needed to do some thinking. Right now, she needed to get out of the car and into the warm confines of the building. "You've fostered parrots?"

"At this point, there isn't much I haven't taken in," Corbin said. "I'm sorry, I must be rambling. And you have errands to run. You don't want to listen to me tell sob stories. I could go on all day with those. Supplies, right? The hard part is that I can't really say. I'm guessing one dog is low on the list of things to sort out for Winton's estate. Let's plan on another week, at least. If I haven't heard anything from a lawyer by then, I'll check in for an update."

The fear that their time with Shadow—Leia—would end soon gnawed at her. She needed more time to figure out how to support Rhett, and while she knew she shouldn't feel this way, she was getting attached to having the dog around. "Thanks. And good luck with that llama."

18

A WARM WHOOSH OF air welcomed Elizabeth inside the store. Sheridan Feed carried everything from cracked corn to bales of alfalfa to an aisle of dog toys.

Elizabeth snagged a shopping cart and dropped her purse into the small front section. On a typical shopping trip, she would bring Rhett. That afternoon, however, she hadn't wanted to peel him away from Leia's return. A deep pit anchored itself within Elizabeth's stomach as she considered the real possibility that Leia could be leaving them sooner rather than later. That her place in the Blau family was far from secure was glaring and clear.

Elizabeth meandered through the aisles. The rows of products spread out before her. She picked up one can and then another, twisting them around to read the facts. Some ingredient lists required a degree in nutrition to comprehend. Those, she put back on the shelf. When she reached for a bag of treats, a conversation from the next row of products seeped between the shelves.

"Shame about your brother. I always liked him."

She heard the crunch of dry kibble bags stacked on top of each other. "Thank you. There isn't a day that goes by that I don't miss him."

"They ever figure out what happened up there? Sad way to go."

"Tragedy, is what it was," boomed a voice. "Sheriff said it looks like he just fell off. Maybe he tripped or a big gust came by. We are all heartbroken."

Elizabeth leaned closer to the racks in an attempt to hear more of what was said.

"You know we'll be there for the service. I still remember your mama's voice in the choir. Sang like an angel. I'm glad she wasn't here for this, may she rest in peace."

"Thank you. We'll see you in the church."

Shuffling indicated the men had departed. Elizabeth was cognizant of her presence as a snoop. She stepped back to her cart, leaning to turn and exit the aisle. One wheel was stuck and refused to move. With a shove, she freed it. The effort sent her and the cart straight into Bobby Black.

"Oompf," she said as the tip of her cart bounced off his. He'd stacked six bags of dog food inside the metal frame. This weight turned his cart into the equivalent of a semi-truck. "So sorry. I wasn't looking. All my fault. Excuse me."

When she brushed his shoulder, an accident she would regret, he put a hand on her arm. "It's no problem. It's not every day I get to run into a beautiful woman buying pigs' ears."

Elizabeth shrugged off the compliment like she wanted to do with his hand. "Studies have confirmed that beauty is truly in the eye of the beholder. Perhaps you have a thing for pigs' ears."

Black laughed, a booming sound. His dark hair and broad chest reminded her of a modern day Gaston. If that made her Belle, she would extract herself from this conversation as soon as possible.

"I like you," he said. "You're funny. Call me Bobby. You must be new in town."

"I am," she said. An offer of her name would only invite more conversation.

"I take it you're a dog lover, too?" He gave the contents of her cart the once-over. The stuffed owl inside a saguaro cactus, training treats, metal bowl, and aforementioned pigs' ears would have brought an obvious conclusion to the most reluctant Sherlock.

Before she could answer, he continued. "I own Black Dogs. We raise championship sled dogs. Were you at the parade on Saturday? I was there with a crew." Pride radiated off Bobby like summer sunshine off asphalt, visible in intensity.

"Didn't see you," Elizabeth lied. She checked her watch to make her need to exit obvious. "Lots of great dogs, though."

His jaw twitched, a slight movement that betrayed an instance of irritation. *I've met many of your type*, she thought. Now to extrapolate herself.

"Black. Oh, I'm so sorry," she said. "You must be the brother of the breeder who died. My sympathies to you." Nothing would quell libido like the mention of death and pity.

The Cheshire grin, spread wide across his face, fell as though shattered. "Thank you."

Elizabeth nodded and prepared to push forward.

Black rolled his shoulders back inside his thick canvas jacket and re-gathered himself. He fished a business card from his pocket and held it out to her. "I'm now the only championship dog breeder this side of the mountain. If you ever want canine advice—or anything else—I'm just a phone call away."

Elizabeth gave him a half smile and pocketed the card. She felt his eyes on her back, her hips, and she exited the store as fast as the checkout line would allow.

19

B AGS IN HAND, ELIZABETH returned to chaos.

A zillion pieces of cereal were strewn across the tile floor of the great room. Tan circles, fruity marshmallows, and tiny pieces of granola were mixed in a cosmic dust across the heavens.

Rhett sat in the middle, scooping up random handfuls before jamming them into his mouth. The dog stood above a pillow, the insides of which were shredded and scattered about. Leia barked at the pillow as though it were possessed. Casey was on his hands and knees in the kitchen. He brushed cereal pieces into a dust pan with his hands while he yelled into the phone.

"I needed you yesterday!"

Elizabeth dropped the bags on the welcome mat and slung her purse over the hook on the coat rack. She scooped up her son to prevent him from eating further dust bunnies along with the cereal. With one foot, she scooted cereal into piles as she made her way into the kitchen.

Casey was shirtless in a pair of joggers. An eight-inch scar snaked up one bicep. A smattering of freckles stretched between his shoulders. He dumped the pan's contents into the trash.

"No, do not put me on hold again. Do not. Ugggh!" Dust pan under one arm, he clutched the phone in both hands and shook it as though he could will the person to return to the line.

"It looks like you've used the cereal aisle as confetti. Everything okay?"

He huffed. "The vacuum died. Guess how I know."

Elizabeth grimaced. She reached for the dustpan. "Let me help."

"We have *mice*." He emphasized the last word with a hiss.

"Mice?"

"You know. Those small, gray, fast little beasts with tiny feet? The kind that eats everything in your pantry and scares the bejesus out of you."

"I know what a mouse is. I didn't know we had them."

"Well, we do. And these people"—he pointed to the phone—"don't understand how quickly I need this situation to be over."

"How can I help?"

Her brother had one foot up, planted on the opposite calf like a flamingo. While music could be heard through the tiny speaker, he watched the floor with hawk eyes as though prepared to leap for the countertop. He waved his hand over the mess, as though he didn't know where to start. "Maybe take the dog outside for a potty break? I'm still on hold."

Elizabeth stifled a snicker as she hooked a leash to Leia's collar and headed to the backyard. When she returned, Casey sat at the kitchen island, hands folded over his head, forehead lowered to the surface. She led Rhett to the cereal-free rug to play with his animal figurines. He animated a brontosaurus, a sheep, and a construction worker while Leia watched the pantomime. In the pantry, Elizabeth found a broom and dustpan and got to work.

The broom made quick work of damage control. She'd found cereal halfway down the hallway to their bedrooms. With a whisk of the bristles, she collected them in the pan. A few pieces had even bounced into the shoes by the doormat.

A rumpled T-shirt was discarded under the couch. She picked it up and draped it over one of the kitchen stools. "When you want to tell me what happened, I'm here to listen."

Casey lifted his head. "Things were going fine until our new friend here found some hoof shavings in the yard."

"Oh. Gross."

"Yup. She snuck one into the house and chewed it up. I got that away from her and wanted to give her a dog treat because I read that's how you show they did the right thing. I reached for the container but knocked the box over when a mouse popped out. It clung to my shirt like a rabid beast. I freaked out and ripped off my shirt which knocked over the rest of the cereal boxes. I think it ran under the couch because the dog jumped on the cushions and started tearing them up. I don't know where it is now, but I do know that if Leia doesn't murder it when it's found I may give up my pacifist ways for the satisfaction of killing it myself."

Elizabeth put one hand over her mouth to hold back the laughter. "I'll get some more cereal tomorrow. Any idea when the exterminator will come?"

He pointed to the phone. "As soon as I find out, I'm heading over to Hart Ranch to see if they have any traps."

Elizabeth threw him his shirt, and he shrugged into it. "Maybe take your slingshot. You know, in case you come under attack on the way."

Casey glared at her. "Hah. Hah. I've got a pot on the stove. Oh, and Nick called me, looking for you. Said you haven't answered his calls or texts. Again. I'm not your answering service, sis."

In the bedroom, Leia jumped onto the bed with Rhett. Elizabeth should have protested, should have distracted the dog with another choice location, but it was too late. Her son, half asleep, flung an arm over the side of the pooch and that was that.

Nick's voicemail only offered further confirmation. "Call me. I have a list of recommendations to go over with you."

20

S HE PUT OFF THE call as long as she could. In the parking lot after work the next day, she dialed the Seattle number.

"Liz. Where have you been?"

"What can I do for you? Your half dozen texts were light on details."

"I'm not going to type what needs to be a conversation."

She could picture him in typical work attire: button-up shirt untucked, sleeves rolled up, a leather bracelet wrapped around one wrist. Nick told her one time it made him feel outdoorsy when he didn't have time to get outside. He would have his third or fourth espresso cup empty at his elbow, residual sugar granules stuck to the bottom. There was a small corner of her heart with an almost imperceptible nugget of tenderness for this man, or at least the memory of life with him. She ignored that twinge. "It's a lot, isn't it?"

"I emailed you a list of potential therapists. Have you looked at those? My mother thinks—"

"When did you send it? I work all day, remember? I can't stop in the middle of class to read a personal email."

"Right. Well, it would be great if you would weigh in on the candidates. I'm going to schedule an appointment for when he's here. Maybe two to get in what we can."

And there it was, the reminder of Rhett's impending absence in her life. Months ago, she'd thought this would be fine. Now, the increasing proximity pressed its hand against her chest. This would be the first time she was without her son since he'd been born.

"Wait. Seattle specialists?"

"They're among the best."

Elizabeth pinched the space between her eyebrows. "That doesn't make sense. If they want to see him more than once, how am I supposed to get him there?"

Nick's voice was gritty. "I'm just doing what's best for our son. He'll be here for Christmas, and I thought—"

"Are you? Or are you doing what's best for you?"

"Liz, we agreed—"

"We agreed to nothing," she said, and hung up.

21

T HE HOUSE WAS EMPTY. Elizabeth headed out toward the
barn.

Inside, two adult figures hunched over machinery. As she
approached, a movement in one of the side pens caught her
eye. A garden hose snaked out from underneath the stall door.
Inside, her son sat in a puddle of mud, his body covered in
brown sludge. The dog, likewise coated, gave a short bark
when she saw Elizabeth. Rhett clapped his hands together,
splattering mud over his face. Every inch of animal and boy
were covered.

Casey kept his barn toasty with the help of machanics. He
swore the nannies made better milk when they were warm
and snug.

Elizabeth's mouth fell open at the mess. "Mommy will be
right back, honey. You stay with Leia, okay?" She pressed her
lips together and crossed her arms to suppress the building
irritation in her bloodstream. Her boots made footprints in
the muck as she stomped over to her brother.

"Casey." Her teeth ground out his name. "There can be
50,000 different bacteria in one gram of soil. Tell me why my
one and only son has far too many of them near his mouth?
Not to mention your plan for cleaning him up before he gets
anywhere near the house."

Casey was up on a small step ladder, his torso plunged into
the depths of the new milking machine. His partner must have
sensed the tension slicing through the air and stayed silent.

"Liz. Hi. This is Rick. He's been helping me all afternoon. Rick, this is my sister Liz." Rick waved but stayed silent. "Forgive her. She's a bit of a science nerd. I'll be right back."

Casey stepped down and headed for the mud pen. Elizabeth followed.

"Things got a bit nuts. It is really difficult to entertain a kid and a dog when you have service people coming out, phone calls to make, and everything under the sun that can break does exactly that. I brought them out here so I could keep an eye on them, and they needed something to do. Look, he's fine. They're fine. It's nothing a hose can't fix."

"I'm not going to hose him off. It's December! He'll freeze."

Casey shoved his fingers under his hat and massaged at his scalp. "Look, Liz. I need to get this fixed. I'm behind in production. The kid is fine. He's having fun. If you want him clean, then go right ahead. I'm a little busy."

Elizabeth turned her attention back to the muddy twosome. Rhett placed a handful of hay on top of Leia. The yellow bits clung to the muck. In response, the dog rolled onto her side, happy to be a canvas.

"Mommy is going to run a nice, warm bubble bath. With the good lavender oils. I'll be right back for you." When outside the barn doors, she added, "Just as soon as I cover everything in the house with a tarp."

22

R HETT SQUIRMED WHILE SHE scrubbed at his scalp, working the shampoo into a sudsy hat. She let him soak in the warm water until the dirt came free from his fingernails. When every inch of her son was scrubbed clean, Elizabeth pronounced him fit for bedtime stories.

Mid-bath, Casey led a washed and dried Leia into the bedroom, one finger hooked under her collar. Without a word, he closed the door behind him. Leia hopped onto the comforter, turned a tight circle, and flopped next to Rhett. With a swift kiss for her son and a pat for the dog, she turned out the light and left them to slumber.

Elizabeth could hear the one-sided conversation of a phone call from down the hall as she slipped into the bathroom. After drying the floor, countertop, and a few stray suds off the wall, she deposited Rhett's muddy clothes in the washing machine. The bathtub, now drained, beckoned her with the promise of a muscle-soothing soak.

Elizabeth's knees creaked when she stood from her crouched position to fumble for her phone. After sending a text, she braved the living room.

Casey, feet propped on the coffee table, had his laptop open, a spreadsheet on the screen.

"Thanks for watching them," she said. "I appreciate it, I do. I'm sorry the milker is broken."

Her brother propped one cheek up with a fist. "You came at the precise moment when I thought I might rip my hair out."

"Can't let you start doing that," she said. "We only have about 100,000 hair follicles on our heads. Those fluffy locks are one of your best qualities."

"Glad to know I at least have one."

A smile tipped the corners of her mouth. She'd been forgiven. Casey sipped from a tall glass and clicked into a web browser.

"I took Jo's suggestion and tried one of those dating sites. She told me, since I'm a grown adult with a decent set of manners and all my own teeth, I have to be able to find someone out there. Makes me sound a bit like a horse if you ask me. Anyway, want to help me work on my profile?"

Elizabeth slid into the spot next to him. "All right, show me what we're working with."

Together, they pored over the half dozen photographs and list of stats he'd entered into the app. After a debate as to whether he should mention his vintage action figure collection, they clicked through the pages of potential dates.

"There's a bit more choice if you're willing to drive to Montana or down to Colorado on a Friday night."

Casey sighed. "Small population equals an abysmal dating pool. Let's search for you. I'm down for a little vicarious window shopping."

"No thanks. I've got the best men in my life right here in this house."

"C'mon. Let's just see what's out there. If you see someone you like, you can make a profile."

"I don't think—"

With a few clicks, Casey removed his filters and added a twenty-five mile radius. The screen filled with pictures of eligible men, and Elizabeth leaned, unable to hide her interest.

"That's the mail guy. He is cute," Casey said. "Oh, and this one is loaded. I redid his kitchen last spring."

Elizabeth squinted at the offerings. It was hard to consider a date with an image.

"Oh, hello. Here's Kade. What happened with you two? This says he's 6'2"—maybe in boots."

She blushed and was glad Casey's attention was turned toward the screen. There wasn't much to tell. There'd been something, and then there wasn't. At least at the moment.

"Hey, it's the Burro guy."

"Corbin?"

There he was, clean-shaven and mid-laugh, a black-and-white photo of him in a vest and bowtie. He sat in a white chair, the back of which was adorned with a gauzy bow. A wedding photo.

"Huh." Elizabeth masked her interest with a question. "Where is he from again?"

"Nebraska. Corn fed."

Relief released the fine muscles in her forehead when Casey moved on. There was nothing wrong with a crush, but it was always better to hide said crush from one's older brother for as long as possible.

Casey scrolled through the remaining profiles. A familiar face drew her attention. She pointed at his screen. "Wait. Isn't that—"

"Looks like it."

A profile for the 45-year-old, wine-loving Packers fan, Winton Black. In a cowboy hat and Black Dogs jacket, he leaned against a fence post, posing for the camera.

Elizabeth's gaze flicked to his relationship status. "It's complicated?"

"Still married, then. Or was. You wouldn't have wanted to go there."

"May I remind you that this search was all your idea? I was just curious what that meant."

"Jo knows the dirty details. Basic sob story, though. Boy meets girl, boy marries girl, girl cheats on boy. Boy ends up alone. Boy dies."

"If they never divorced, then wouldn't the girl inherit everything?"

23

E LIZABETH CHEWED OVER HER conversation with Casey, like a pencil between her teeth. For all she knew, Winton and his wife had legally separated. She'd walked that road herself, and it was complicated.

In his jammies, Rhett stacked Casey's many throw pillows into a makeshift fort. When one fell, Leia snapped for it and tugged at the fabric. Elizabeth snatched each pillow away. The mouse incident had reinforced the wrong message.

A scroll through the local news sites revealed nothing new about the case. Elizabeth tossed back the remains of her glass of lemonade and crunched on a mouthful of ice. Like a jigsaw puzzle missing a piece, the picture didn't quite shake out. She needed a distraction.

"Hey, Liz."

A cube slipped down her throat, and she choked, spluttering into the receiver. "Sorry. Hello."

Corbin laughed. "You okay? It would be awkward to get a call from a friend only to hear them choke to death over the line. "

So they were friends. Interesting.

"I'll be fine, thanks. I'm calling because Leia is starting to chew on things. Expensive things. I know things are a bit up in the air with her at the moment, but we don't want to reinforce that habit. Also, I don't actually know what I'm doing when it comes to training a dog. Or most things in life, really."

Corbin laughed. The photographs from his dating profile flashed in her mind. 39. Avid snowshoer. Animal lover. Big fan of sci-fi.

"It's totally cool. We're all just doing the best we can here. That's why we need each other."

"Thanks for that reminder."

"I should have asked—what is she chewing?"

After an extended conversation about why dogs choose certain items for chew toys, what she could use to soak up that energy, and how trauma shows up in dogs, Elizabeth had a growing list of things to research and an expanding crush on her new friend.

"Oh," he said. "My office assistant said some official paperwork came. My guess is it's about Black's estate. I don't know what it is yet, but I'll get into the office in the morning and let you know."

"Thank you."

"My line is always open for a friend."

24

"I OWE YOU FOR this. Big time."

"Sure. Happy to help out." Kade Michaels wiped his hands with a rag before he accepted the leash, dog attached, and a bag of gear from Elizabeth. "I've been hoping you'd call. Didn't know it would be for this."

Rhett lunged for Leia, and Elizabeth struggled to balance him in her hip. "I really appreciate it. Jo's in Missoula and Casey has clients. After the last couple of days, we don't want to leave her alone for long. I've got to get Rhett established with a new pediatrician here because according to my insurance company we can't go to a specialist until a regular doctor has evaluated him and so I had to take a day off work—"

Kade placed his hand, warm and strong, on Elizabeth's arm. He waited to speak until Elizabeth lifted her gaze to meet his. "Hey, it's okay. We'll be fine. What are friends for?"

There was that word again.

The garage was filled to the rafters with activity. When Elizabeth had arrived, she'd found Kade consulting a water-stained text on vintage Plymouths. In the closest bay, a '44 coupe waited, hood raised like a gaping mouth. In addition to the regular run of brake work and transmission flushes, Kade's Garage expanded its projects into restoration fanatics. People from all over the county and beyond, bringing him their 4-wheeled, prized possessions. Business was booming.

A familiar black van was lifted in the farthest bay. Kade and Elizabeth watched a tech step underneath to poke and prod its underside while consulting a tablet.

"I'll be right back." Kade headed toward the tech, Leia following the lead. "Raj, hold up on that one."

Elizabeth leaned Rhett closer to the window of the coup to check out the interior. Smooth white leather, polished woodwork.

The two mechanics whispered back and forth before Raj nodded and Kade returned.

"Sorry 'bout that."

"Everything okay?"

"Yeah. We just found a personal item in the vehicle. My policy is to get a hold of an owner before we move anything. Cover our bases. This particular customer can be intense."

"Pretty sure I have a half dozen bobby pins I've lost between the seats. Should I fish those out, so you don't have to call the cops over an oil change?"

Kade smiled. "Hair accessories are fine. Unless they're solid gold, we'd never notice them."

25

C ONCENTRATION WAS IMPOSSIBLE AT the pediatrician's office. Two seats away, a little girl bashed the head of a dolly into the hard plastic arm of her chair. A little baby screamed while his mother attempted to breast-feed him. The television blared an animated flick intended to distract. Multicolored blocks and toy cars flew from the toy bucket as a trio of toddlers set in on its contents.

Rhett watched the movie, one fist stuffed in his mouth, the other moving in a rhythmic pat on Elizabeth's thigh. He'd had little exposure to other kids. The chaos was endless. She gave a silent prayer of thanks when Rhett's name was called.

The nurse, practiced and clipped, pelted Elizabeth with a barrage of questions. Like a robot, she answered, mechanical and dry. This conversation would only end in one conclusion, and Elizabeth need only wait to receive it. The doctor would come, repeat the exam, and give her anything other than immediate hope.

She'd heard it all before, read everything she could in every imaginable, reputable book or magazine about babies and how one begins to speak. Boy babies often took longer to start speaking. Two was longer than average. Older kids who struggled to speak may have different learning needs. May need specialized support. Therapy. They'd just have to see, be patient.

Rehashing all of this made Elizabeth's stomach flip. She willed herself to remain calm and open to the new doctor's opinion.

When the nurse stepped out to locate the pediatrician as promised, Elizabeth selected a book from a tub underneath the examination table and read it to Rhett. Twice. She let him experiment with turning the pages and checked her phone.

A text from Kade.

With a flick of the screen, she revealed an image from the garage. In the foreground, Kade knelt in front of Leia. With one finger, he balanced a tennis ball on her nose. The dog's eyes were focused on the ball, her posture stiff and alert.

Kade: She has skills!

Elizabeth: Very, very impressive.

Kade: We'll keep at it.

A soft tap on the exam room door signaled an incoming interruption.

As her thumb slid across the screen to lock it, she recognized the emblem on the van behind Kade. Black Dogs.

Deputy Ryland on his phone, standing beneath.

Black Dogs. Personal items. Found in the van.

26

B ACK AT THE GARAGE, the van was gone.

"Oh good, you're here!" Kade burst from the office when he saw Elizabeth. "Let me get Raj."

Elizabeth peeked at the paperwork in piles on the desk. Diagnostic results in shades of green, yellow, and red were printed for customers. None had the name Black.

"Can I help you find something? "

"I was just thinking how much your printouts look like the report cards we send home with kids."

Kade cocked his head, an approximation of an Australian shepherd assessing a field of wily sheep.

"Everything distilled down to colors. You know, all the bars and charts." *You're drowning here, Liz*. "Anyway, speaking of kids, how is Benny doing? "

Benny, one of Elizabeth's former students, had lost his mother in a tragic shooting a couple months prior. With a father out of the picture, his care had been transferred to his uncle. Elizabeth missed the precocious little boy.

"As good as can be expected, I think," Kade said. "He's asked about you a bit. Doing okay at his new school."

"Please tell him I said hello and that I miss him."

Kade nodded. He was a fierce protector of his nephew. Witnessing the little boy's grief had to be a struggle.

"So we got her to do it. By the way, we fed her a ton of treats to make it happen. She might not be hungry for dinner."

Raj brought Leia in and handed the leash off to Elizabeth. Kade got down on one knee in front of the dog and held the fluorescent tennis ball in front of her nose. Elizabeth was so close, she could see a tiny razor nick on the underside of Kade's jawline.

"Okay, girl. You know what to do."

Everyone watched as the car mechanic set the ball on the end of Leia's nose. He held it there for a moment before releasing his fingers from its surface, one at a time. When his last finger lifted, Leia made micro-movements with her nose to keep the ball balanced.

Raj threw both hands up in the air and yelled, "Good girl!"

Rhett clapped his hands together, and Elizabeth set him down to hug the dog. Leia leaned into her youngest fan and licked at his face.

"You did all this in one day?"

"It was pretty incredible. To be fair, the job we thought would take up the afternoon was held up, so we had time to spare. But yeah, pretty awesome. It's like she was born for training."

Elizabeth scratched between Leia's ears. "You'll have to give me trainer lessons." She wanted to ask if the client was Black.

"Makes me think about getting a shop dog."

"Holding you to that," called Raj. He snagged a mug from a workbench and headed into the small office area. "Nice to meet you all."

Elizabeth waved at the retreating tech. When she turned around, Kade was watching her.

"You know, you can call me for more than dog sitting."

Her insides melted into a pool in front of her feet.

"I...it's...the changes have been so fast. I'm getting used to a whole new school. And Rhett..." How could she explain her worry that whatever they had, she would mess it up? She needed her life in order before imposing her baggage on someone new. She didn't want Kade to be a rebound. He deserved more. And then there was Corbin.

Kade nodded, slow and thoughtful. "I get it. It's okay. There's a lot going on. And I'm focused on Benny most of the time. Don't worry about it. Call me anytime to dogsit. It was fun."

"Kade, I—"

Before she could stumble through an explanation that it was her, not him, that he was quality, a solid rock with whom she wished she could spend her time, he'd followed his coworker through the door and was gone.

27

"I'VE BURNED THROUGH ALL my favors."

"Oh stop. You still have me. When I'm in town. You said she did great with Kade. Between your friends, we can cover you," Jo said.

"Don't think I don't appreciate it. I'm just in this weird place right now."

The two women chatted in Jo's cozy kitchen. Jo squatted in front of the oven while Elizabeth watched from her seat.

With gigantic blue oven mitts on each hand, Jo opened the oven door. A savory aroma filled the kitchen.

Elizabeth smelled rosemary, thyme, and the earthy umami of porcini mushrooms. Her stomach rumbled, an audible engine coming to life. "What piece of heaven do you have in there?"

"Mama always called it Mountain Stew. I kept the basics, added some of my own pizzazz, and voilà!" Jo lifted the lid of a Dutch oven to reveal its bubbling contents. She pressed the button for broil and closed the oven door, leaving it open a crack. "Last step is to brown the cheese under the broiler."

"I'm going to need that recipe."

"And I am going to need details as to what happened at Kade's. Clint won't be home for half an hour, and I've got an open bottle of red that deserves appreciation."

"You can pour mine into a plastic cup," Casey said. He poked his head in from the living room. "I think the three of us here are heading out to the barn during halftime. Leia will need a break, Rhett will want to bring the donkey an apple, and Buck will never forgive me if I don't say hello."

As a modern day goat herder, Casey had a soft spot in his heart for the animals, even those with a well-known reputation for stubbornness.

"Let me guess. The performer is some cute, twenty-something blonde in the equivalent of spandex underwear?"

"It's as if you know me," he said. Jo handed him two sippy cups, one with wine, one with water, and he ducked back out the doorway.

Sunday supper had become a Wolf House tradition. What had started as a casual invite blossomed into a standing event. Sometimes Elizabeth or Casey would bring over the main meal but most times, Jo cooked. She waved off their offers with the excuse that Clint loved leftovers for the work week.

With her brother out of earshot, Elizabeth detailed her awkward conversation with Kade.

The two men were far from enemies, but they weren't exactly friends, either. Their tangled connections with the Hart family put Casey and Kade at odds in loyalty. Anything close to a friendship would take time—and a miracle. Talking romance with a sibling was problematic to begin with. Adding rivalries, infidelity, and murder made it downright inadvisable.

In the spindle back kitchen chair, Jo crossed her legs and leaned forward to rest her wine glass on the table. "So, you're telling me the opening you've been waiting for happened, and you blew it?"

Elizabeth bit her lower lip and nodded as her ears flushed from a combination of wine and embarrassment. "Pretty much."

Jo shrugged. "Eh, who hasn't been their own worst enemy sometimes?"

"Thanks. Now I feel worse."

"You know that's not my point. Here." She slipped off the mitts and reached for the pen and pad of paper that were never far from her side. Jo was a woman who believed in an accounting of a life through notes. "Let's make a list of all the reasons you should take it slow. Then we'll make a list of all the reasons you should throw caution to the wind, ditch the kid on your brother, and head over to his house right now."

"There's reason number one why not right there. I don't know where he lives. In fact, I don't know much about him at all. What little I know is tied up in a really complicated set of relationships. We talked about my car. That's not exactly a launching point for romance."

"Noted." Jo scribbled on one side of the pad, then drew a line down the middle. She tipped the wine bottle toward Elizabeth's glass and then her own. "All right, now something in favor."

Elizabeth looked out the window, then at the floor, then to Jo. "Okay, I'll just say it. He's hot, and it's been a while. "

"H-O-T." Jo spelled out the word.

"That makes me sound shallow. There's more to him than that."

"Hold that thought," Jo said. An oven mitt went back on each hand. She pulled the casserole from the oven and set it on the range top to cool. Jo hooked the oven door with one foot to close it, ditched the mitts next to the sink, and returned to her seat. "All right, where were we? Oh yes, Kade Michaels is what my gran would call a prime stallion."

Elizabeth snorted just-sipped wine out her nose. "Jo!"

"What? She was a horse breeder. She would be the last Candelaria to shame anyone for honesty."

"Okay but it's more than the way he looks in a pair of jeans. He is a good listener. And I mean he truly listens, without his own agenda. That night when we talked, I felt like his only goal was to be there for me. I don't know if I've had that before."

"Not Nick? Or Justin?"

"Nick has grown—some—but he'll always be a narcissist. He only listened to assess how much I knew of his sleaziness. Justin was sweet, but I think his situation was too crowded to have room for anyone else's issues."

Jo nodded, adding to the list. "What else?"

Elizabeth ran a finger around the lip of her glass. A fine, high hum sounded out, pure. "I've got a kid. That complicates things."

"It does. So does he. There's empathy in that."

"How about the fact that he owns his own business and likely his own place, and I live at my brother's house and still don't know what I want to be when I grow up?"

"That's hardly your fault."

"Isn't it? I can't seem to convince myself otherwise."

Jo set her pen down and put her hand over Elizabeth's. "Look, we fly and we fall until we learn the way of things. Being your own enemy won't make the ride any easier."

Elizabeth released her wine glass to wipe away one tear and then another. Jo squeezed her hand before releasing it to take a swig from her own glass.

In the living room, boots scraped the mat at the front door. Keys dropped on a hall table. A moment later, Clint brushed into the kitchen. A five o'clock beard shadowed his face, dark circles undercut his eyes.

"I've got a decent bottle open. Another in the rack. That stuff we had at the Sanderson wedding."

"Better not, thank you. Ten to one odds say I'll be called back within the half hour."

Jo, mid-pour in a fresh glass, lifted the neck of the bottle. A drop splashed on the tablecloth. The red liquid violated the sunny, yellow fabric.

"Would you prefer to drive past the kitchen window, and I could hand you your supper in a sack?"

Tension squeezed the points between Elizabeth's shoulders. Her eyebrows drew together, and she looked at the stove, her feet, into the glass. Anywhere but at the source of the perceived rift. A witness to a childhood of marital spats, this was a reflex.

"Only if you put a toy inside," Clint said.

He and Jo burst into laughter. Clint bent down to kiss his bride with an audible smack. She grabbed his chin with both hands and kissed him back.

"Fine. More wine for us."

Adrenaline dissipated from Elizabeth's bloodstream. Her comprehension of relationships had been curated over years. The fear of conflict became an armor forged in the name of self-preservation. Dating was one thing. Subjecting a good guy to her inability to function in a healthy relationship was another level. Insecurity couldn't be flipped off with a switch.

"Is our favorite future cowboy here?"

"He's in the barn with Casey," Elizabeth said.

"Better say hi now." Clint elbowed the screen door open, then swiped a biscuit from the basket staying warm atop the stove.

"Hey!"

Clint grinned and held up the biscuit. "Add it to my bill."

Jo called out to his retreating form, "Make it quick. I want to know what's stealing my husband from a proper meal."

28

"**H**E SAID IT AGAIN."

Casey mouthed the words to Elizabeth as he handed Rhett over.

Clint rummaged in the cupboard for a box of dog treats. "All right chaps, what flavor will it be—bison, bacon, or...vegetable?" The box depicted a smiling Labrador.

In front of Clint sat two golden retrievers, practiced in their patience. Each offered a brief tail wag across the tile floor.

Leia was a new addition to the Sunday night pack. Her brown eyes vacillated between the model dogs and the purveyor of treats.

"Pretty sure this one's a lady, Sheriff," Casey said. He scratched Leia between her ears, and she sat on his feet.

"Good girl!" Clint presented her with a cookie. She gobbled it up.

Elizabeth set Rhett down and held out her hand to Clint. "Could I have one of those?"

Clint held out the box, and Elizabeth fished out a bone-shaped treat. She knelt in front of Leia and placed the biscuit on the bridge of her nose. Leia's pupils lasered onto the snack.

"Okay, girl!"

At Elizabeth's call, Leia flipped the treat into the air and caught it. With her chomp, the audience clapped and offered congratulatory pats.

"Dog," Rhett chimed in. He clapped once, a smile from ear to ear. "Dog!"

Jo raised her eyebrows at Elizabeth. "Let's wash our hands and eat while it's hot. We'll have to celebrate with ice cream after."

"I think I can facilitate hand-washing," Casey said. He took his nephew's hand and guided him toward the living room.

With the toddler out of earshot, Jo set a hot plate at one of the place settings. "All right, husband, spill it."

The old oak table held eight, and she kept it set at all times. Known for hospitality and a willing ear, the Wolf household often had an extra guest or two. A cheery, burlap table runner graced the length of the table. At its center, a wicker cornucopia held a few decorative pumpkins and ornamental corn cobs from the month before.

Clint shoveled a mouthful of steaming stew into his mouth and chewed. He wiped his mouth with a napkin and checked his watch.

"You've got time," Jo prompted.

Clint took another bite and closed his eyes in appreciation. "Wife, this is heaven. As per usual. Could I trade you a second biscuit for the information?"

"A plea bargain? Deal."

"Should I...er..." Elizabeth navigated the complication of having a law enforcement officer for a friend through reminding him she was present.

Clint finished chewing and then ran his tongue along the inside of his lower lip. "It's public knowledge. About to run on the Billings evening news." The nearest city was the source of the closest major broadcast to Sheridan County. "We're opening an investigation into the death of Winton Black. That's why I think I'll get a call here any minute."

"New evidence?" Jo plopped a second biscuit on his plate.

"Yup. We found signs of a scuffle. A chair knocked over. A mug broken on the floor. There's also a fresh chunk of wood out of a front step."

Jo frowned. "That's a stretch. Could have been a lot of things."

Elizabeth's focus volleyed between the couple. They batted facts back and forth in a practiced match.

"It could. Wallet's missing, too."

"You think it's a break-in?"

"We need time to figure out what we think. That and for the snow to melt. We've got the place corded off. Bringing a team up from Laramie to help."

Jo set a plate in front of Elizabeth, then another at the setting next to her. She returned with a small portion of stew on a plastic plate. Jo blew across its surface a few times before placing this in front of Rhett's booster chair. "Better now than try to go back in time and recreate a crime scene. Anything else?"

"Maybe. In a pocket, we found a photograph of an old rickety cabin at the edge of a lupine-covered meadow, a dog whistle, and a solid gold dog tag that matched one we found in his van."

Bingo.

The jangle of Clint's work phone alerted him from within a coat pocket. "That'll be the press."

"Just in time for dinner. It was lovely to remember what you looked like, if only for a brief moment."

"Anything for you, my love." With another kiss, he left to retrieve his gear.

"I'll get the boys." Elizabeth pushed her chair back to stand. One foot caught on the chair leg, and she winced, sucking in her breath.

At her yelp, Leia leapt up from the kitchen rug to inspect Elizabeth for damage with a few pointed sniffs. The dog nosed her hand, then leaned against her leg.

Jo watched the exchange. "I think I may have a solution to your little issue."

"Which one?"

29

"YOU GOT PERMISSION FROM the school board?"

"Direct and express."

"Just so long as we're clear." Maggie regarded the scene before her, one foot angled out from the other in an approximation of a ballerina in third position. She hovered there, in the hallway, as if willing herself to avoid involvement until her own role was clear. "Can't have parents calling, up in arms about allergies and fleas."

"Mrs. Wolf told me to send any complaints her way. Want to offer her a treat?"

Maggie grunted. "Maybe after I get the kids. I just washed my hands."

Elizabeth's other coworkers gushed over the new addition to the staff.

"Isn't she the cutest little snookums-face!" Rita rubbed Leia's belly, blowing her kisses. The dog dropped to the tile to offer herself for adoration. "What a love! Do we get to keep her?"

Elizabeth frowned. Her singular pushback to Jo's brilliant plan was the risk that everyone would get attached to the new scenario—Elizabeth included.

"Short answer? Not sure. For a bit, at least. I've got to figure out how to introduce her to the kids."

Rita smoothed one hand down Leia's length. The dog closed her eyes in gratitude.

"Got it. How about we tell them she's a guest teacher. Talk a little dog biology. Have them label a diagram. We could also talk about the responsibility of caring for a pet."

"I like it. I'll comb the library for any books we could use."

"Cool. I'll hunt through my vocabulary units. And I can totally walk her during my prep time."

"You don't have to—"

"I want to. It will give me an excuse for some fresh air. Otherwise, I sit in the break room, drink stale coffee, and stare at my phone."

Between the volunteers, gaps in her schedule, and the possible interest of students, Elizabeth figured out a dog walking schedule.

Jo had wondered if Leia would make a good therapy dog. Animals that can be trained to provide emotional support are in high demand in schools, she'd told Elizabeth. If Leia completed a formal program, she could become an official service dog.

"Then you could take her to work with you. The kids get amazing support, and you have a place for her to be during the day. No favors necessary."

"I love this plan. I do. I'm worried the kids will get super attached. Then what?"

By kids, Elizabeth knew she was thinking about Rhett, most of all. That morning, she'd found Rhett babbling to the dog. She was unable to pick out words from the chatter, but there were definitely sounds. New sounds. Sounds that could become formal speech.

What would she do when they had to give Leia to her new owner?

30

A WEEK OF SUCCESSFUL school days rolled out before Elizabeth.

Leia was beloved by everyone in a matter of hours. There was never a shortage of attention as Leia enjoyed the status of honored guest at the school. That moment, she was outside with the lower grades, paying close watch to swingset negotiations while two students brushed her. Still held back by her healing leg, the students lavished her with pets and sympathy between their games.

The fifth graders organized a turn-taking system in which they doled out time holding the leash. She overheard one little girl offering a chocolate chip cookie from her lunch in trade for extra brushing time.

Other than their guest teacher, the biggest buzz that week was the annual Carol Night. Each year, students from the school choirs and local performers gathered at the WYO Theater to sing. The event was a popular fundraiser for the food bank.

"Lights?"

"Check."

"Ribbons?"

"Check."

"Tinsel?"

Elizabeth ducked her head down from the attic storage space to reply. "Didn't they outlaw that stuff?"

"Good point. Still. Tinsel?" Jo waited, one foot on the bottom rung of the rickety ladder, list in hand.

"Just a sec..." Elizabeth rustled through more boxes of decorations, old fitness equipment, and abandoned technology. "Check. Also, I think there's an inflatable Frosty up here. Whatever it is has a pipe, a hat, and what I hope is a deflated carrot. There are also two of those plug-in, wire reindeer that light up. Maybe three. It's tough to tell where one starts and the other begins. Want me to drag one out?"

"I remember those. Got them at a garage sale. The kids like to make costumes for them. Last year, the buck was Batman. The Cape hid the lights, though."

"They don't look too heavy," Elizabeth said.

Jo wrote Frosty and Reindeer (x3) to her list. "Yeah, go ahead and hand me a Rudolph. I can bring one of the shop lights over to check out the rest."

Elizabeth had volunteered to crawl up into the blackness that morning in the hunt for decorations. Jo was on the decorations committee for Carol Night and wanted to take stock. Elizabeth adored her friend's default to lists and regiments.

"I think I'm going all the way up with the flashlight. I don't want to pull on the wrong box and cause the stack to topple."

"Be careful! Only step on the rafters. Our forefathers built that ceiling, it's so old."

Elizabeth grunted as she shuffled a short stack of boxes toward one side. She filled a plastic crate with the smaller items and lowered it through the opening with a pink jump rope. "It's the garland. Nice and light."

Jo received the package and untied the knots. "Where did you learn to tie all of these?"

"My dad, some. An afternoon binge-watching videos for the others."

Jo freed the rope and set the box aside. "How is the new dog arrangement working out?"

"Kids love her. My coworkers love her." There was a pause. "I love her."

"A normal response."

"If this was a normal situation, I wouldn't feel so guilty every time a kindergartner wraps their arms around her neck and whispers, 'I love you, Leia' into her ear."

"Good thing dogs don't have an ego. Well. Most dogs. Who's watching her tonight?"

"Casey. He said the carolers are always off-key and the wine gives him a headache."

Jo pitched an eyebrow. "Hey, I helped pick those bottles. They are perfectly decent, right out of the Willamette Valley."

Elizabeth shook her head. "I wouldn't take it personally. He's avoiding an ex, I think. One of the community choir members."

"Oh! Yeah. Abraham. That didn't end well. A dog is much better company. "

"I don't want to give her back, Jo." Once she'd said the words out loud, Elizabeth was relieved and ashamed. She popped her head back through the hole. "Am I a jerk for saying that?"

"An honest one. But no, not really. You'd be questionable in my book if you didn't fall for her."

Elizabeth nodded, then her face was gone again. In its place came a reindeer, the rope a noose around its neck.

"Not its best look, I know," Elizabeth said. "Seemed to be the least fragile point."

"You may be right about that. For the deer anyway."

31

R HETT GAVE A SOFT coo at the sight of the building, bedecked with trimmings. The WYO Theater was a Sheridan institution, heading the business district for decades. The
Art Deco facade stood out among its plain brick neighbors.
A longtime location for everything from art shows to country
hoedowns, the building had shepherded a variety of talented
artists into the local spotlight. Lost opportunity? *Check.*

Elizabeth watched as her son took in the sparkles around
the room. Each choir was in charge of a section of the building, tasked with choosing decorations that represented their
songs for that night's concert. Stage right hosted a bevy of
menorahs, from vintage silver to an LED-lit entry. Stage right's
stair railing was looped with boughs of holly. Each of the
cocktail tables clustered in the lobby had a different, thematic
centerpiece. Rhett lunged at the six plastic geese when Elizabeth leaned close enough to set her plastic cup of red blend
on the tiny surface. She transferred him off her hip and to the
ground. He ran over to a fabricated palm tree propped near
the restrooms. Elizabeth hurried after.

At the base of the tree, Rhett paused, his head tipped back.
Elizabeth followed his gaze to the trunk above him. Hundreds
of miniature lights wrapped around every inch of the tree.
From afar, the tiny lights emitted a soft glow. Up close, the
effect was a subtle color shift, a pattern of shifting shades. The
browns transitioned to white, the greens to a soft blue, then
yellow and then back again. As though a living organism, the
lights gave the display a hypnotic energy.

"Bat!"

Rhett's voice startled Elizabeth. This was new. This was a development.

Over their head hung a small, stuffed bat, its feet wired to the underside of a palm frond.

"A bat—yes! Great job, buddy!"

They'd spent a few sunsets that fall watching the bats from Casey's back yard. Dark shapes flitted in and out of the twilight, their deft hunt a show against the navy backdrop. Elizabeth and Rhett had tucked themselves into the deep, wooden deck chairs with mugs of hot cocoa and blankets in order to watch the mammals at work.

Emboldened by her cheer, Rhett smiled and repeated his new word. "Bat. Bat."

"Yes, a bat. I guess I thought palm trees were more for monkeys."

A laugh boomed behind them. Elizabeth squeezed the wine cup, startled.

"Don't spill it. Terrible stuff but the line is too long to wait for a replacement."

A tall man in a long-sleeved, emerald shirt, its front divided by a line of shiny, silver buttons, held his hand out to Elizabeth. A flash of bright white teeth accompanied his greeting.

"I'm Eddie. Eddie Enos. It's nice to meet a fellow bat enthusiast."

Eddie waved at Rhett. In response, the boy pointed up and then looked back at Eddie. "Bat!"

"He's...learning his terms," she said. Why did she always excuse her son? She'd considered it a protective measure at one point, a cushion between him and a cruel world. *It's me, though*, she thought. *It's my own shield, not his.* "Rhett loves animals. Everything about them, don't you honey?"

Rhett smiled and pressed his hands to the trunk of the palm.

"In that case—" From inside his pocket, Eddie procured a plastic seal the size of a bottle cap. He held it so Rhett could see, then handed it to Elizabeth. "Would you be interested in taking care of another friend of mine? Definitely not one for the trees. He's a little guy, though, so I'll let your mom keep him safe until it's playtime."

Elizabeth accepted the tiny animal, its dark gray back a smooth hump. "Thank you, Mr. Enos."

"Eddie, please. Call me Eddie."

"So, this is your tree?"

Eddie stepped back to appraise his work. "It is. Took me a couple hours and an app to make it happen."

"It's gorgeous. The bat was an unexpected touch."

He laughed again. "Not where I'm from. The hoary bat is one of only two native mammals on the islands."

"Which islands?"

"Hawaiian."

"You're a long way from home." Elizabeth wanted to inhale the words back inside her throat the minute they'd left her lips. "I'm sorry, that's a stupid line you probably hear way too much."

"I do, but I am far from home."

"Ms. Blau, hello. Good to see you. And Eddie! Nice to see you, man." Detective Ryland clasped hands with Eddie. "So glad you made it again."

Eddie gave the officer's hand a solid shake and clapped his other hand on the man's shoulder. "No uniform tonight?"

Ryland, a lean man with long limbs, reminded Elizabeth of her high school calculus teacher who could fit his entire body through a wire clothes hanger. His long, pianist's fingers pointed to the jaunty fedora atop his head. "I'm undercover, can't you tell?"

"Where, 1920s New York?"

Elizabeth watched their exchange. *Old friends*, she thought. Their banter was easy, like waves lapping between opposite banks.

Ryland kicked one heel out, his trouser cuff revealing tartan socks in his polished shoes. A vest hugged his shirt, a bowtie ringed his neck. He wore the outfit like a second skin, and Elizabeth had the sudden urge to see his closet. She pictured a clear split between highway khaki and bootlegger button-ups.

"Respectable man out on the town, no matter the decade. I've missed you, man. Staying long?"

Eddie crossed his arms to regard the deputy's outfit. In contrast to the vintage look of the deputy, Eddie was a model off a runway. The crisp lines of his denim ended in spotless dress shoes, ankles bare. His left hand was covered in silver rings, two on multiple fingers.

"Long enough to collect. You know I won't suffer this atrocity you call winter a day more than necessary."

Elizabeth tented an eyebrow. "Why would you leave paradise this time of year?"

Eddie turned his beaming smile to Elizabeth. "Family pride, that's what."

"Now I'm really curious."

"There's a story there, for sure," Ryland said. "I'll leave you to tell it. Looking forward to the show tonight, Eddie. A beer before you skip town?"

"Count on it, my friend."

"Will I need another glass of wine for this story?" Elizabeth's cheeks were flushed, whether from the wine or the chance to extend her time with the handsome stranger, she didn't know.

Eddie glanced at a giant timepiece wrapped around his wrist. "Let me get you one. Anything for our young biologist?"

Rhett had busied himself applying crayons to a picture of a snowman, a cardinal perched on his top hat. "How about juice?"

"I'll be back before you can miss me."

Elizabeth watched the man join the line. She enjoyed the tingle that traveled her spine. *Careful there.*

"Well, hello again! Elizabeth, right?"

Elizabeth didn't associate the sing-song call with herself until she felt a hand wrap around her forearm. "Alma, the filmmaker. Remember me from the parade?"

"Oh, hi, yes. Sure."

Alma chattered away like a motivated squirrel. She commented on everything from the displays to the adorable sweater Rhett sported. Elizabeth spared a wan smile for the woman but kept her eye on the concessions.

In line, Eddie was almost to the front when a woman with long, red nails tapped a talon on his shoulder. He turned, his ever-present grin lifted to meet a friend, only to have it drop like a lead weight. Eddie said something to her, so quiet his lips barely moved. Her wide grin faltered at the edges before she reinstated it with a determined narrowing of her eyes. She maintained the gleaming show of teeth as he replied. The person behind the counter called for the next in line, a knife slice through the tension, separating Eddie and the woman.

After an interaction with the bartender, Eddie formed a triangle with the three drinks and slid them off the counter, clenched between his fingers, and headed Elizabeth's way. The woman watched him leave, glaring daggers at his backside. Turquoise sequins scattered over her top, a pile of wavy beach hair spilled over her back.

Interesting.

"Hello," Alma said, as she extended a hand toward Eddie. She waved her cameraman over from the shadows. He approached with the camera on his shoulder, red light on. "I'm filming a documentary in the area. Would you care to be interviewed for a possible spot in the film?"

"No, thank you." He brushed past Alma, elbows out. In front of the woman, he set a beer on the table before he handed the other drinks to Elizabeth. "At the counter, they asked if I wanted a straw. I guessed yes. Glad to see I was right."

"A lid is a blessing most days. Thank you, again."

"My pleasure. Now where were we?" Eddie blinked a few times as he sipped at his beer, as though to rid his mind of recent visions.

Alma hovered nearby, then shrugged at her camera person and they moved off to chat up someone else.

Elizabeth sipped at the wine. When the acid hit her tongue, she grimaced. "You were going to tell me a story."

"Ah, yes. And it's a good one."

"Liz, hey, sorry to interrupt." A harried Jo approached their table. "Any chance I can swipe Rhett for a few?"

"Uh...of course."

"Thanks, hun. I need a guinea pig to test out my cookie decorating station. You're okay if I sugar up your kid before I give him back, right?" Angled so only Elizabeth could see her, Jo flicked her eyes toward Eddie and then lifted her brows to indicate her duplicity.

Elizabeth's toes tingled at the suggestion. This man lived an ocean away, but she sure could relish a little alone time with him. "Is there any other way?"

"Not with Clint manning the gumdrops. Back before showtime. Looking forward to your set, Eddie." Jo whisked Rhett off to the other side of the lobby.

"Guessing Jo Wolf is a friend of yours, too?" Eddie said.

"I've yet to meet an enemy of hers."

"There's been one," Elizabeth said. Jo had told her the origin of the small, hairline scar left from her altercation with a guilty forest ranger the day Buck saved her life.

"I suppose every story has one." Eddie set his cup on the table. "You asked what I was doing so far from home, but that question is more important to ask of my great, great, great-grandfather."

"I'll bite. What brought him out to the middle of a neighboring continent? The exact middle is in North Dakota, of course." Elizabeth swirled her wine in her glass. She enjoyed the easy conversation with this man. This could be a speed date, she thought, and committed to enjoying every minute. "That's over seven hours in an airplane now, I can only imagine back then."

Eddie interlocked his fingers, knuckles stacked. "He and his friends were paniolos, Hawaiian cowboys. They came all this way to become champion ropers at the 1908 Cheyenne Frontier Days."

"Incredible."

"It really is, when you think of what it must have been like to be an islander among a sea of lilies back then. Not that it's much different now."

They both scanned the crowd, the bulk of which represented the state's predominant current inhabitants.

"Were there a lot of Hawaiians in Wyoming?"

"Not many, but more than you might think. We came across the ocean and into Washington, Oregon, and beyond. Looking for jobs, for land, for a new life. Some stayed. Our history doesn't often make the textbooks out this far. I think that's part of why Uncle Jack came out here. He knew he had serious talent, knew he was just as good if not better than most, and shot for the moon."

"So they won, right? That is a good story."

"They did, and it is, but that's not why I'm here."

Whether it was the wine, the snug environment, the recessed lighting in the lobby, or the warmth in Eddie's eyes, Elizabeth wanted to be closer to this man. She shifted her stance a little closer. He smelled of cedar and a hint of citrus. "Please continue."

"Back home, people celebrated the three winners for days. There were parades, parties, and dances in their honor. Papers all over the United States shared the news. These guys were heroes to many. But not to everyone.

"At events, the white cowboys would talk all kinds of trash to the paniolos. Morning, noon, and night, people would yell at them, spit at them, threaten them. I think great gramps must have known they were small people, scared they would be proven to be lesser cowboys. Still, that's incredible pressure to withstand."

Elizabeth was quiet, listening to Eddie talk, but a flash of that sequin top pulled her gaze from his eyes. Over his shoulder, she saw the rebuffed Alma bump into the woman who'd been in line with Eddie. Alma signaled the camera person and began to speak into her mic.

"Where'd you go? Am I boring you?"

"No. Not at all. I'm sorry. I thought I saw Jo coming back with my son. With Rhett. You know, like the Baader-Meinhof phenomenon."

"I don't...but I think I get it."

The venue's speaker system crackled. "The show will begin in five minutes. Please finish any food and beverages and make your way into the theater for a wonderful show."

"I'd better get to the crux of things," Eddie said. He tossed down the dregs of his beer and swallowed.

"Well, the paniolos had enough. In one confrontation, Jack bet one hundred thousand dollars that he would beat any man in the arena."

Elizabeth spluttered her sip of wine. "That's a lot of money now."

"It is, and it was. I don't know what he was thinking. He sure didn't have it, even if he won. Maybe he thought they'd be long gone before anyone came to collect."

"So, what happened when they won?"

The smile was back, in full effect. "He must have taken pity on the loser. Either that or he figured the other guy was cash-strapped too. At any rate, in front of the local sheriff, they agreed to one hundred annual payments of one thousand dollars, the first payable then and there."

The crowd dispersed on their periphery. People fished for tickets in their pockets, tossed cups in the waste bins, and ushered children into the theater. Alma and the woman were gone. A few people clustered near the doors.

"So, you're here...?"

"For a payment. Yes. The last one, too. Though there's been a bit of a snag. Then I'll be on my way, the debt settled."

Elizabeth did the math in her head. "But—"

"You're about to say it's been more than a hundred years, and you'd be right." He stacked his empty cup into hers and scooped them up with the cocktail napkins. "Travel wasn't cheap, especially over water, but I guess the promise of a witnessed debt for a grand was worth the initial expense. Each year until his death, Jack came back for the money. Forty-two payments worth. When he died, his son took over, and so on. There were a few years here and there when no one came."

"World War I and II?"

"And Vietnam. Then things would settle down again. Trips would resume, generations took over."

"Forgive me for asking, but the trip over here has to be about that much if not more, isn't it?"

"It can be. It's a point of pride. For my family, it's about what's due, what was earned. I suspect for the kin of the loser, too. They pay to show they can, that the debt was never a hardship in their history."

"I doubt that," Elizabeth said.

"Maybe, but that's not my side of the story to tell."

He held out his hand, and she took it. Eddie squeezed her hand in both of his. "I've enjoyed this. I hope our paths cross again."

"Me too. One last question?"

"Shoot."

Elizabeth wrestled with her thoughts. Ask him what he's doing after the concert. Ask Jo to babysit. Ask him if you can visit him in Hawaii. Ask him something, don't let him go!

"I'm a bit of a science nerd. You said the bat was one of two native mammals to Hawaii. What's the other?"

"The monk seal." With a wave, he headed backstage.

32

THE BURST OF APPLAUSE when Eddie took the stage was an indication of his popularity. Stage lights sent streaks of blue through his black hair as he tuned his guitar. He perched on a single, maple stool in the spotlight and adjusted the microphone.

"My people have been coming here for a long time, and I am proud to be welcomed by all of you. As you may have heard, I haven't come here to sing Christmas songs as that is not my heritage. In case they haven't taught you this in school, white people colonized the islands, stripping what they didn't like from our people and inserting their own traditions. I've brought a few traditional tunes of my people to add to your holiday celebrations, not take away. I like to lead by example, you see."

The crowd tittered. From her seat in the tenth row, Elizabeth could see a hundred faces aglow in the stage lights, rapt attention on the man in front of them.

"Why talk about the past, though, when I could sing about it?" Eddie smiled and began to play.

His voice was clear and strong, the depth of which would reach the farthest seats without amplification. The first song was about a girl who sailed the islands and upon her death became a breeze that brought her people home. Next, he sang about a battle, lost ways, and sorrow. The room was silent on the last note as the audience held its breath.

"This one is a gift for my new friend." He winked in Elizabeth's direction as the crowd cheered and with deft fingers, began a Django Reinhardt tune.

Jo leaned over to whisper in her ear. "Friend, eh?"

For his last song, he played Home on the Range, but in Hawaiian. The performance was beautiful, melodic. When he finished, the crowd erupted in applause. People were out of their seats, crowd-sourcing a standing ovation.

"Thank you, Sheridan. I've loved sharing my music with you."

After Eddie, multiple elementary schools trotted out their cutest students in matching holiday attire to sing classics and a few pop versions. The county community choir sang a tribute to Nat King Cole, a capella, and the high school drum line followed with a Blue Man-inspired collection. The show was a rousing success, but it was hard to top Eddie Enos.

Elizabeth had him on her mind as she waited in the lobby, gripping Rhett's hand tightly and waiting for Jo to return from the restroom. Eddie's palm tree glowed from its corner.

Enid pushed out from the theater doors. She wore a deep navy tunic over silver leggings. She shrugged into an oversized, puffy coat and began to wrap a houndstooth scarf around her neck. When she spotted Elizabeth, she wove through the crowd in her direction. "Hey there, how the heck are you?"

"Better than I deserve. You?"

"Can't complain. Business is always booming in December. I head home every night to soak my feet from running around all day. Waiting for Jo?"

Elizabeth nodded. *Also for Eddie*, she thought.

Jo made her way over to them, wiping her hands on her pants. "The ladies room is out of paper towels. I let someone know."

"Get your hands off me!" An explosion of fur coat and perfume exited the theater into the lobby, followed by a pair of ushers.

"Ma'am, the show is over. It's time to go."

"I wanted to finish my drink!" A hand with familiar red nails held a flask above her head, as though to play keep-away from the ushers. "I'm a widow, dammit. I'm in mourning.

She spat the word out, like a bug swallowed from atop a motorcycle, then whirled to face Elizabeth, Rhett, Jo, and Enid.

"Hello, Hannah," Enid said. "Enjoy the show?"

The woman huffed at them, then spun on her heel to head out the door. A perfume of flowers and desperation floated in her wake.

"That," Jo said, "was Hannah Black."

33

"**M**ARRIED TO WINTON BLACK?"

"None other."

Facts clicked into place for Elizabeth, the edge pieces to a jigsaw puzzle. The woman couldn't have been more than forty-five. The highlights of her curls were bottle-born to blend away grays, but a few wrinkles betrayed her years.

"No wonder she's upset."

Enid scoffed. "Hah. She threw a party at the news, knowing her."

Jo shot Enid a look, then turned to Elizabeth. "Hannah wasn't a faithful wife. He found out, and she moved to Billings."

"I see. Did they get divorced?"

A man held open the front door for his date. A few snowflakes floated inside past them to land on the carpet where they melted at Elizabeth's feet.

"Not that I'd heard. Or that Gary's heard." Secrets didn't stay secret long in that community. If they hadn't heard it at Beans, it wasn't the truth. "Might have been one of those arrangements people make to avoid technicalities."

"You mean lawyers?" Elizabeth could sympathize. She paid a monthly whopper of a bill to Stanley, Reitz, & Whalen.

Enid took a pair of gloves from her purse and slipped one over each hand. "I wondered if she'd be back for the funeral. I guess that answer is yes, but why?"

34

T HERE SHE WAS. HAPPY. Secure in herself. Smug. Who did she think she was?

It was obnoxious, really, to see someone like that. Pretty but no peacock. Nothing that couldn't be found in a dozen women. Confidence. What would it feel like to crush her, slap that smile right off her face?

There'd been time to study her before the show. She'd done her hair. No doubt the scent of honey and orange blossoms wafted from those tresses. Anyone within a half dozen feet could likely smell it, but not from back here. Not when one was wedged behind the table on which a stack of fallen toy soldiers lay, post battle. Their blank faces and haphazard arrangement belied a loss. The wounded and dead left until it was safe to come crawling back for them. Empty, black dot eyes pleaded to be returned to the field upright, for a chance to fight again.

"Don't worry, little friends, I'll avenge you."

A belch nearly gave the lookout away. The alcohol wasn't kind to a tender stomach. The sulfites made one's skin hot. The burn did nothing to cool a temper, to ease an ache. Acids churned alongside an underdone country fried steak. This town was a torn billboard from yesteryear. A place anchored in the past like a vase from a guilt-driven bouquet of roses.

It wouldn't be long now. Maybe a few days. Tie things up, put this place in the rearview mirror. Too long there'd been a link, a chain.

If only her face hadn't disrupted the night. Thrown plans for a loop. It wouldn't take much, though, to get it all back on course. Getting into a car too late at night. Taking the trash to the curb. On a hike. Accidents happen.

At first, the guilt from the tussle with Winton was loud, a roar in the ears that wouldn't allow sleep. A week had gone by, and this sensation lifted. The future, free from Winton's influence, his rules, his stupid dog, was a beautiful place. When you really wanted something, when you set your very purpose to it, what was one little bump in the road to a lifetime of success?

There was one loose end left to tie. One voice that needed to be silenced.

Then the past could stay the past.

35

S TUDENTS LAGGED IN THEIR lessons, half asleep from the candy and late bedtimes the night before. Elizabeth sipped at her third cup of coffee. Only Leia, ever-ready for adventure, sat upright at the front of the classroom, tongue lolling as she watched the kids in their seats.

From the hallway came the scent of a cedar diffuser. The addition of aroma oils came with the weekly visit by a district school counselor. Elizabeth thought the intrusion verged on the border of car air freshener but said nothing. Well-meaning people rarely appreciated an interruption of their perceived good work. Elizabeth cracked the classroom window for fresh air.

A weak sun promised a break from winter weather. Piles of snow glittered in the sunbeams. A few chickadees hopped between the branches of nearby spruce trees. Elizabeth turned to address her class.

"You know what? How about we get some sunshine with a little extra recess?"

Like a garden watered after a drought, the students cheered and lept from their seats to grab coats and pile outside. Elizabeth shouldered into her own jacket and looped a whistle around her neck to follow the students, Leia close at her side.

Students swung between the monkey bars, squealed at the static from a trip down the long, plastic slide, and kicked off from the swingset, gleeful legs reaching for the gray sky. Leia ambled out to a sunny spot, soaking up the few winter rays.

Elizabeth smiled, her soul warmed by the simple joy of the moment. *We must do this more often.*

Leia lifted her nose from the sidewalk as Clint's patrol car eased into the parking space next to Rita's wagon. The sheriff reached into the passenger's seat, stuffed papers under one arm, a clipboard under the other. Students watched his every move. One student dribbled a ball, several clung to the chain link fence. All waited.

Leia, upright now, gave a short bark of recognition through the fence. Elizabeth met the man at the gate. She lifted the bar to let him in, then let it fall in place behind him.

"What can we do for you, Sheriff?"

Leia sniffed at his hand. He looked down at the dog, then knelt to pet her. The shoulders of his coat sloped, heavy. He met Elizabeth's eyes for a moment and then looked away. He pressed his lips together, and his bushy mustache sagged in defeat. With a brush of his hands onto his pants, he stood to face her.

Elizabeth whispered under her breath, "Clint, you're scaring the kids." *You're scaring me.*

With one hand, Clint removed the packet from underneath his arm and cleared his throat.

"Miss Blau, I am here to serve you paperwork demanding you return one Chinook dog by the name of Princess Leia of Alderaan, registered to one Black Dogs, LLC, to the rightful and proper owners according to Sheridan County jurisdiction. You have seven days to relinquish the dog to the rightful owner."

Gasps echoed out from behind her as Elizabeth's face blanched. Leia whined and thumped her tail.

Under his breath, Clint whispered, "I'm so sorry, Liz."

36

A UTOPILOT IS A COPING mechanism. Elizabeth didn't know how she made it home that night, let alone what she said to her coworkers or the students for the remainder of that torturous school day.

When the bell rang, she collected Leia, her lunch bag, and her keys. Next thing she knew, she sat in front of the television as pictures flashed on the screen. The numbness settled within her being, a weighted blanket.

Casey moved around her, like a flitting moth in search of a resting spot. At each pass, he'd offer something. A pillow for her back. A pour of their latest experimental stout from the keg. A hug. He'd played with Rhett, fed him, and whisked him off to bed without comment.

At midnight, her brother gave her a baleful look, turned off the movie she hadn't watched, and went to bed.

When the house settled so that even the dust was still, Elizabeth blinked away a single tear.

Her laptop lay on the coffee table, the task of lesson planning abandoned. Work would not happen tonight. Could not happen tonight.

An idea tugged at her mind, and she reached for the device anyway. She typed two words in the search bar. The screen lit up with results.

The Chinook breed was newer and rarer than most. Out of New Hampshire, an explorer and adventurer bred his pet with sled dog racing in mind. Through intentional selection, he established a breed that was fast and athletic with an excellent temperament. The Chinook are work horses with big, loving hearts, their DNA a story of dedication. What first appeared to Elizabeth to be some kind of mutt was in actuality a tried and true sled dog. A breed of incredible value and far from common out west.

Elizabeth followed a tangent in her next search. Black Dogs rose to notoriety not only for their ability to raise quality sled dogs, but because they had the unusual breed, among others, to offer. Winton and Bobby leveraged the unique in order to build an empire in their industry.

A bang, like the sound of a kicked metal drum, shook Elizabeth from her search. The blindingly bright yard light blinked on from its pole-top height above the barn.

Elizabeth's heart raced at the sound. She clenched her hands, digging fingernails into her palms to will calm back into her thoughts. Anxiety began to unravel its grip on her rigid pose when a second bang rang through the night.

She rose in a fluid motion, cat-like, and lifted Casey's rifle from above the door. Its weight was a solid assurance in her hands.

The dark hallway hid her shadow as she made a quick check of the bedrooms. In her room, Rhett snoozed in his twin bed, covers kicked off, arms stretched up above his head. One dinosaur pajama leg was flung over Leia. The dog snoozed at his side. At the sight of Elizabeth, the dog shifted as though to rise from the bed. "Stay there, girl," Elizabeth whispered. "I'll be back."

With a soft click, she closed the door. The cream hallway tiles glowed in the light from the yard, an eerie hue. Across the hall in Casey's room, her brother lay flat on his back, still dressed, his snore at top volume. He'd finished his beer, then hers, and poured himself a third. The high ABV of the stout meant he was conked. The door made a snick behind her.

Back in the hallway, Elizabeth stooped to collect the small flashlight that hung on a hook next to the door frame. A playground whistle dangled from the handle strap. Elizabeth peered out the window into the backyard.

A dark figure moved among the shadows near the barn. It sniffed at the toppled garbage can. Debris was scattered across the soft earth. The shape shifted to inspect the inside of the can, and a massive paw rolled it like a plaything.

The whistle. Elizabeth slung the rifle behind her back, cracked the back door, put the small metal mouthpiece to her lips. She aimed three blasts out into the night.

The big cat swiveled its head toward the sound. Elizabeth slammed the door shut and threw the bolt. With a sniff of the air, the cougar slunk off into the dark.

Elizabeth pressed her back to the door. She exhaled the lungful of air she'd locked within her rib cage and sank to the floor. Relief pooled in front of her feet.

When she'd moved out west, Casey warned her that her adopted state was more wild than not. That out here, nature came first and human safety came second, if at all. Sure, one could carry bear spray, bullets, and bravado, but there would always be surprises that tore through a false sense of ease.

An avid backpacker since her youth, Jo took Elizabeth out on the trails, pointed out signs of wildlife, helped familiarize her new friend with the flora and fauna of the area. She told Elizabeth that predators preferred to maintain distance from people more often than not. But when food sources were added to the equation, situations get dicey.

Cougars didn't hibernate. The sleek mountain lions did often change their diets to fit the season, shifting to eat what was available. Raccoons could have toppled the can, unaware that the big cat watched for its opportunity to pounce.

With an exhale, she pushed herself up off the floor to get ready for bed.

Her eyes hit window level just in time to see a car, headlights off, back out of the driveway and speed east.

37

"**C**AN IS THE OPERATIVE word here."

"How so?"

The burble and hiss of an espresso machine came through the speaker. Elizabeth had called Casey's lawyer at first light.

"You can petition the court to keep the dog based on its need for medical treatment, needed for it to recover from the condition in which you'd found it."

"Her."

"Of course. Bobby Black has a claim, but it's a shakey one, and you have some space to make your own. You could claim that she is yours since you took possession when the owner died. Or hell, try to claim that Winton gave her to you before his death. You do have options, some better than others."

"All of which will cost me."

"Money and time. That's what it comes down to. And really, time is money in my world. I'll give you the family discount, but something like this is tough to predict. I've pulled a few files when we handled livestock, not domestic pets. Wyoming, Montana, and a couple in Colorado. Since the invention of sophisticated tagging devices, many are open and shut cases, at this point."

Elizabeth slumped in the chair and bit her lip to think.

Sleep had remained elusive. She'd tossed and turned, rising every hour to double check the locks. Each time she crossed the floor, she'd rationalize what she'd witnessed. The driver of the car lost track of time at a friend's house and got turned around trying to get home. They pulled over to check a map but didn't want to shine headlights that could wake a household.

None of these assurances transformed her jangled nerves into a rational calm.

A phone call to Casey's trusted legal counselor first thing in the morning gave her footing in regaining a sense of control, however fleeting.

"Could we work on this in phases?" Elizabeth thought of the money she'd been gifted from Justin's estate. The ten thousand dollars, less some initial brewing equipment purchases, bulged in her otherwise tiny bank account. She told herself it was seed money, an opportunity to fund her own brewing business and jumpstart savings for her own place. Would she carve off a chunk of that security for the potential of a lost cause?

If it meant a chance to keep her son talking and her family intact, absolutely.

Stirrings from the bathroom indicated Casey was awake. She'd need to rouse Rhett soon. Take Leia out for a potty break. Make everyone scrambled eggs. Pretend all was fine.

Part of motherhood was shielding children. You wanted them to turn into smart, capable people who could take on life's challenges, head-first. But the world could be a cruel place, and sometimes life wallops a person unaware. Scars were left on young hearts.

She couldn't protect her son from every heartache, but in this moment, she was far from helpless.

"What would a grand buy me?"

"A portfolio of hope in the form of research, witness statements, and an official letter with legitimate bite."

"Do it."

38

WHATEVER ELIZABETH HAD EXPECTED, it hadn't been this.

A scene from an old western ringed the drive. Mercantile on the left, a dentist and other offices in the middle. Even a saloon held court to the right. Behind these structures were a dozen smaller cabins scattered in the outfield, each with its own fence. Most held a burro or two, but a red roan pony hung its head over the nearest homestead fence line. Oversized ears for its short body, the equine watched Elizabeth with interest. A dog lay in an enormous oval bed on the porch of a neighboring home, a passel of puppies nursing along its side.

Honking from a flock of ducks sounded from behind a milner's shop. An improvised pond had been set into the ground nearby. Bright orange extension cord connected to a floating deicer on the surface of the water.

A rooster flew to the top of the squat church's bell tower. Its comb a crimson flag, it strutted along the roofline, inspecting the visitor.

The door to the blacksmith's shop opened. A figure backed out, an enormous bag of chicken feed slung over one shoulder. The person removed a rope from a nail in a post and stepped off the porch before they spotted Elizabeth.

Corbin startled at the sight of her, and the bag slid off his shoulder and into his arms. He staggered under the shift of weight before he managed to set the bag upright against a hitching post.

"Sorry. I'm unannounced, I know. I tried calling. Thought I'd come by on the off chance you'd be here. I'm in a bit of a time crunch. I can come back."

"I think I read somewhere that a heart attack first thing in the morning builds stamina," he said, one fist clenched to his torso. It was an attempt to defuse the tense moment, but Elizabeth could see the rapid rise and fall of his chest. With a grunt, he hefted the bag back onto his shoulder. "Well, welcome to Burro Buddies. Come on, I'll show you around."

Elizabeth followed him to the doors of the saloon where he lifted a bar that held them shut.

Up close, the buildings were small but impeccably detailed. The saloon had front windows with elaborate shutters, a balcony with brightly colored pots, and a bench outside. Each porch beam was hand-hewn, the swinging doors a fresh shade of hunter green.

"This is...not what I expected." Elizabeth stepped inside the saloon and into a veritable poultry hotel. Like an office mailroom, two sides of the room were filled, floor to ceiling, with cubbies. In most, a hen held court. From atop their nesting material, each watched her pass.

Corbin extracted a handful of cracked corn from a pocket. With a wave of his hand, the golden kernels scattered in the filtered light. All around her, hens took flight. Wing flaps filled the air. They descended upon the offering and devoured it within minutes.

"You should see them go after a container of mealworms."

Elizabeth shook her head and scrunched up her face. "Ew. Let's not"

Corbin tipped up one corner of his mouth. Elizabeth was close enough to see flecks of gold in his irises.

"Ducks next?" Without waiting, he ushered her through the side door. This opened into another room with access to the outdoors beyond. The pond, snug against a brace of cottonwood, held a few beautiful waterfowl making use of its depths.

"You don't keep that door closed?"

Corbin flipped open the lid of a plastic bin and scooped out some feed. "I do at night. Ducks are more complicated than chickens, I think. The more freedom I give them, the more they come back to visit."

"So, they aren't rescues?"

A mallard waddled over to Corbin. The man offered a handful of the meal. "Some were. It's not just chicks people buy at Easter only to abandon when they grow up. They don't all stay, but a few do."

"Guess it's the heat lamps." Elizabeth held her hand under a red bulb anchored to a post with a clamp. With a flip, she warmed her palm.

Corbin shrugged. "Could be. I heat the pond, too. Give them food. It's not a bad place to overwinter." He ventured a gloved finger to stroke the emerald feathers of his houseguest.

"Casey wants to come back as a duck."

"Oh, really?"

"He wants to be something that can walk, fly, and swim. What else is there in life?" Elizabeth squatted near Corbin to watch a female join her mate.

Corbin had his sleeves rolled up, a stocking cap pulled down over his ears. Tufts of hair curled at the collar of his flannel shirt. December was months away from the sun-kissed days of summer, but Corbin's cheeks held tight to coppery sunsets.

"I have someone I want you to meet."

He held out his hand to Elizabeth. She put her hand in his, and he hoisted her up.

"I'm always happy to meet someone new."

Corbin chuckled. "Lulabelle isn't a person. Though she can be better company than many of them."

They headed for the small cabins behind the mock town. Elizabeth noted that each was actually a single barn stall with an attached corral.

"Is this Lulabelle?" As they walked past the first tiny home, Elizabeth reached out to stroke the muzzle of a pony.

"That's Reggie. He's a boy," Corbin said.

"Whoops. No offense, Reggie." *Smooth, Liz.*

A crowing sounded out across the yard. "And that's Rex. He's always showing off for guests.

Elizabeth wondered how often people came by this sanctuary. "Did you know that a T. rex's closest living relative is the chicken? Ostriches, too."

Corbin paused outside a gingerbread cottage with red trim. "That explains a lot. Spend enough time watching chickens and you can see it in the way they stalk a worm." He extracted a handful of carrots from his back pocket and held one out to her. "Here we are. Elizabeth, meet Lulabelle."

With little warning, a fluffy white head with long lashes framing deep-set eyes peeked out from the barn stall. Having sighted the carrot Corbin waved about like an orange semaphore, the rest of the long-necked, four-legged creature followed.

Big yellow teeth crunched down on the proffered vegetable. As she chewed, Corbin took the opportunity to peek inside the stall, check the water trough, and wiggle the gate latch.

Elizabeth was mesmerized by this animal. Taller than herself, Lulabelle stood on dainty footpads with huge, black toenails, snowy wool thick along her sides. "She's lovely. Where did she come from?"

"Ida Moran, out of Ten Sleep. A cool lady. She rescued Lulabelle to accompany her on hikes, like a pack animal. Took this girl everywhere until Parkinson's made that impossible."

"I didn't know Burro Buddies rescued so many different animals."

"That's the thing about rescues. There are never enough, and even fewer that specialize. We all do what we can, when we can. This is my first camelid." Corbin took a comb from his back pocket and stroked the sides of the animal with a light, practiced touch. "If I keep working with her, she may stay sweet. Won't let me get too close though, yet. Might be a male thing. It's a shame, too. Ida had this sweater for the winter months."

On a peg hung the garment. Elizabeth lifted it from the nail. "Maybe she prefers the company of women, nothing personal. Can I try?"

"If you like." Corbin stepped out of the enclosure to give Elizabeth access to the animal. Hands on hips, he waited.

As she reached out one hand to touch Lulabelle's side, slow and steady, Elizabeth said, "Llamas aren't known for being snugglers."

"How did you identify her? I didn't give the species on purpose. There may be a plate of cinnamon buns riding on your answer, no pressure."

"Seems big. And see the horns?"

Lulabelle kept one beady eye on Elizabeth as she rested the winter jacket against her bulk. It was as though the llama debated whether the threat of clothing was worth the sacrifice of further carrots.

"Size aside, she has a longer face. A rougher coat. I'm no expert, but I'd love to hear the final verdict."

"You're in luck as I have a specialty vet coming up from Cheyenne next month, a buddy of mine."

"A rescue facility doesn't have anyone local?"

Corbin scoffed. "Of course I do. Couldn't keep my license if I didn't. Most large animal vets around here specialize in equine and bovine, though. This one has exposure to more of the exotics. Mark and I were Huskers together. He'll confirm it."

"So, how do cinnamon buns factor in?"

Corbin raised an eyebrow. "Jo and I have a little wager over Lulabelle's genes."

Elizabeth laughed. "So, whose side am I on?" Elizabeth tapped at the dirt with the ball of her boot.

"My lips are sealed." Corbin mimed a zipper across his mouth and chucked the imaginary key over his shoulder. "I'm impressed with your knowledge of South American mammals. Might have room for a ringer on our trivia team.

Elizabeth laughed. "When you're a science teacher, you pick up a lot of facts. That's all." She didn't explain the embarrassment of a habit in which you spout off said facts when nervous. It had been enough work to keep details of the relative sizes, diets, and wool values of the Camelidae Family from escaping her lips.

"Humble, too. The other teams won't see you coming." Corbin stuffed his hands into the now empty back pockets of his jeans. "Enough of my sideshow. You came here with an agenda. How can I be of service?"

39

"Т HAT IS A COMPLICATED situation. It happens, though. A person dies without a will, the animal is brought to me. Out of the woodwork comes a relative with a claim. Sometimes, after I've adopted them out. Those are the worst."

"What happens?"

Corbin crossed his arms and kicked at the dirt with one boot. "We have to follow the law. Even when it doesn't feel great."

"That's awful."

"You've got Charlie, though. Ain't a better lawyer around. If there's a way out, he'll find it. Keep you from getting banged up too much in the process."

Elizabeth took a deep breath then exhaled through her nose. She'd need to keep her strength to get through the emotional gymnastics. "Thanks for being honest. I'd rather have that than false assurances. I do have some questions, though. Official ones."

Corbin nodded. "I've got some coffee in the Doctor's Office. Let's talk there."

On their walk back, he pointed out more features of the facility he'd constructed. Elizabeth listened to him explain the planning behind the decoration.

"It all started because I needed special stalls and kennels for animals that couldn't handle being housed with others. I called it the jail as a joke. One winter, I was socked in with some extra lumber, old paint, and too much time to myself, and the official Jail front was built. From there, the rest were a matter of completing the town."

They passed the Feed Store, a front for his food storage facilities, and stopped at the steps of a white-washed building. A sign declared this building to be the Infirmary.

Corbin brushed mud from the soles of his boots onto the rough mat and stepped inside. He stopped at the sink near the door to wash his hands, taking time to scrub them pink before a rinse and a towel-dry. Elizabeth followed his lead.

The inside had the appearance of a small veterinarian's office. One small room held a metal table and shelves of supplies including bottles and jars of all sizes and shapes. Another room with a large glass window had a wall of metal kennels of various sizes. The front room held a desk, a chair, a tall file cabinet, and a second table on which rested a coffee pot. Corbin opened the top drawer of the cabinet to extract a mug and a handful of packets. He poured the pile of sugars and creamers into a hill on the desk. Elizabeth watched him fill the mug from the carafe and hand it to her.

"Help yourself to mix-ins. My thermos is back at the stable. Back in a jiffy."

Elizabeth rifled through the offerings for her cup and then looked for a spoon. On the sparse desk sat a computer, a phone charger, and a book with a pen clipped to its side but no other implements. With a glance at the door, she crossed to the cabinet and opened the top drawer.

A bag of ground coffee, a few boxes of decaf black tea, a basket of sugars, a carton of creamers, and a box of fettuccine were jumbled together in the drawer. No spoon.

Elizabeth was about to give up the hunt when she spotted a photograph tucked behind a few open envelopes jammed at the back. She pulled back on the paper with one finger to reveal a picture of Corbin next to a blonde in red-framed sunglasses. The pair sat on a granite boulder on a creek bank, the sun shining overhead. He'd hooked an arm around her shoulder, his head turned to plant a kiss on her cheek. She laughed at the camera person, the picture of mirth, yet one hand was on Corbin's as if to push it off her shoulder. Elizabeth recognized that woman.

Footsteps on the porch alerted her to Corbin's return. With a clunk, she closed the drawer and returned to her perch on the desk.

Elizabeth held up her cup as he entered. "Any chance you have a spoon?"

"Oh, of course. I'm off my host game today. Visitors aren't too common. It's usually just me and the animals." After another hand-washing, he opened the drawer and withdrew one of the long sticks of pasta. "Long lasting and biodegradable."

"I'll try anything for science." Elizabeth stirred at the contents of her cup as Corbin poured his own. "Uh, what do I do with the...stir stick?"

"Just a sec." Under the table hummed a mini fridge. Corbin opened the door to withdraw a compost bucket. She tossed her noodle into the blue, plastic bucket, and he returned it to the cool interior of the fridge.

The side of the small appliance was tiled with photographs of people posing with animals. Dogs were the most frequent subjects, but there were a few with pigs, chickens, and a cat or two.

"Hey, is that Jo?" One of the pictures was of a woman holding the halter of a soft-eared donkey, a goat in the background.

"Yep. From August. I got lucky there. Rather, Buck did."

"You must get to know a lot of people."

Corbin shrugged. "Part of the job. For better and for worse."

Elizabeth blew on the steaming liquid in her cup before she ventured a sip. "It's good. Hot, but good."

He blew into the mouthpiece of his own tumbler before venturing a sip. "It's not a fresh pot, but I made a big one. I was up early feeding kittens."

Elizabeth took another sip. A strong brew with a hint of sweetness, and she tasted caramel. "It's great, thanks. Kittens, eh? Bet they are cute."

With a wry smile, he took another drink. "They make them that way so you tolerate waking up every couple of hours to deal with their incessant meowing." He gestured at a rolled up sleeping bag wedged behind the door.

"I was wondering—how well do you know other people who work with animals?"

"Like in general? There's a lot of us. Has to be, in a place where so much still depends on them. Most are okay. Some are saints, some are devils. A typical mixture for humanity."

Elizabeth looked down into her mug, the swirl of cream a thin streamer in the pale brown. "Did you know Winton Black?"

"Ah. I knew smart, charming women didn't drop in on bachelors for kicks."

Heat flushed Elizabeth's cheeks.

Corbin continued. "Yeah, I knew him a bit. Not as much since he made it big. Seemed he and Bobby were too wrapped up in business. Decent enough guy. Big heart. Had some cool plans he was trying to work out. Would have liked to see how it all turned out for him. Why do you ask?"

Elizabeth swallowed. "The vet who checked out Leia after we found her said she had some old injuries. Was concerned she may have been abused."

"Huh. Not likely. Winton wasn't like that. Maybe the vet hadn't seen a sled dog before. They can get a bit banged up in the sport."

"So I'm learning."

Corbin set his tumbler on the desk, then turned back to the cabinet. From inside the second drawer, he extracted a pamphlet which he slid across the desk surface toward Elizabeth. "A few of us who run rescues put this together. It has an overview of animal cruelty laws in the state and steps to take if you find evidence. Burro Buddies is listed on the back with the other agencies."

Elizabeth unfolded the paper to reveal legalese and phone numbers. "Thank you."

"All of us have our facilities inspected. Even for-profits like Black's. The licensed ones, anyway. I've only been to his place once. Up the mountain a bit. Even if he wasn't the good guy I knew, their kennels were top notch. Clean, secure. Lots of employees around. He was proud of his setup. Invited us all to see how he could keep so many animals healthy and still turn a profit. Black wanted to set the industry standard and had plans riding on their reputation. He wouldn't have risked that."

40

E LIZABETH ENTERED BEANS WITH a head full of thoughts to unpack as well as a belly full of subpar coffee to counterbalance.

Gary offered something akin to a gingerbread latte, but Elizabeth's stomach turned at the thought of anything else sweet. She asked for an americano and a ginger snap instead. When she'd explained subjecting herself to terrible coffee in order to chat with an attractive man about important topics, he gave her a look of pity—and the coffee on the house.

In a corner booth, she nibbled the crisp cookie alongside the tidbits she'd learned about Winton. The spicy warmth eased her insides.

Corbin said Winton was a professional, someone who wanted to establish better business practices. He'd mentioned Winton had big plans, ideas that wouldn't see the light now that he was gone.

She'd also seen the picture from Corbin's drawer. Though she'd tried to push it out of her mind, all she could see was his arm around the slim shoulders of Hannah Black.

Elizabeth unfolded the brochure again and spread it in front of her like a placemat. Pictures of animals packed into shelter facilities, baleful eyes turned to the camera. A map of the state, yellow stars scattered across to note no-kill rescue facilities. Alphabetized phone numbers below the picture.

She ran her finger across the entry for Burro Buddies.

"Looking to adopt? I've got some connections." Alma, mug in hand, took the seat across from Elizabeth. She pursed her lips, assessing, then frowned. "Or are you looking to place?"

"I'm not looking to adopt—or place." From the counter, Gary raised one eyebrow at Elizabeth, the subtle gesture of an occasional bouncer. She gave a short shrug of one shoulder, as if to indicate she'd yet to determine her need. "Can I help you?"

"Oh. We met at the parade. I'm Alma—"

"I know. You're making a documentary about sled dogs." The sentence landed with a bitter note. Elizabeth was surprised by her own tone, but she'd wanted a quiet place to think. Alma opened her mouth, as though to respond, then closed it, trout-like. "Sorry, that came out a bit harsh."

"No, I'm the one who should apologize. I spend so much time in reporting mode I forget what it's like to talk with people. Like having a normal conversation is a luxury I've forgotten how to enjoy."

Elizabeth regarded the woman. Five or more years younger than herself, Alma wore her hair in two long braids, a fleece headband wrapped around her head. Hiking boots topped with snow pants and a long-sleeved Henley gave her the look of a skier back at the lodge in search of a hot toddy.

"I need a refill. Can I get you anything?" Alma scooted her chair back to get up.

"Thank you, but if I have any more coffee, someone will have to peel me off the ceiling." Seeing Alma crestfallen, Elizabeth added, "How about peppermint tea?"

Alma nodded and stepped up to the counter.

Elizabeth looked back at the brochure. She dug out her phone and searched for llama rescues. None in Wyoming.

Before she'd left the rescue, she'd asked Corbin what would happen to their new friend. He said in an ideal situation, a specialty adoption agency would take over, place her with good people. Sometimes there was funding to transport animals.

"And when there isn't?"

"People like me do our best to place them. It's tough, though. Those who spend all their time with one type of animal really do get to know what makes them tick, what would make for a good home situation. They have better connections. This is my first llama rodeo."

The rattle of a cup on a saucer brought Elizabeth back from her memory. Alma set the saucer in front of Elizabeth before she sank into her own chair. The steam from Alma's cup fogged her glasses. She flipped them onto the crown of her head before reaching for the pitcher of cream. She poured a healthy dose into the mug. "It's a bad habit, I know. But I can't stand the stuff otherwise. By the way, the guy at the counter says to wink three times if you need help."

Elizabeth shot Gary a look. He held up his hands to her. "He's kidding," Elizabeth said. "He's a friend of mine. Knows I've had a long week."

"Eh, I'm used to it. People aren't always happy to see me coming." Alma lifted her cup to her lips and held it there, thinking, then shrugged. "You could say it started with a chatty seven-year-old who refused to mind her own business. Give her a camera and a full ride to film school and you create a monster."

"Scholarship? Impressive."

"Thanks. For my application, I exposed a local cat food cannery. If I hadn't gone to college, I think I would have had to spread my wings anyway, if you catch my drift."

Elizabeth nodded. "The truth hurts sometimes."

"As it should, for some."

The cold edge to Alma's voice hung in the air between them.

"I was surprised to see you around. Feels like that parade was ages ago. I would have thought you'd taken your footage and headed back to...uh...?"

"Oh. We didn't intend to stay. Had to clean up some unfinished business. Ian and I are about to take off, though. You'll see us again for the race. Assuming it happens."

Elizabeth frowned. "I hope it does. I've been looking forward to it."

Alma sucked in her cheeks and probed the bottom of her mug with her eyes. "Have you?"

"I have. Gary over there, too. Has his own sled. He's from Alaska and sled dog racing is big in his family."

"I see," said Alma. Her fingertips pressed so hard against the mug they turned white. "I guess I wondered if they would still have it after the death of Winton Black."

The mood had shifted from friendly ease to a chilly withdrawal. "I didn't know him, but I'm told he was dedicated to his dogs. I'm guessing he'd wish the teams all good luck if he were here."

"My gram said there's no such thing as luck, only accounting for our choices."

Elizabeth blinked at the woman, unsure what to say.

"If you'll excuse me," Alma said. Her chair scraped against the stained cement floor of the shop. She unhooked her pack from the back of the chair and ducked out the front door.

Gary came over to collect the abandoned mug. "What did you say to her?" The string of paper snowflakes hung over the door still swished in Alma's wake.

"I wish I knew. Seen her before this season?"

They both watched as Alma mashed the crosswalk button and tapped a foot as she waited for the light to change.

"Nope. Showed up at the parade with that camera guy. Made a reference to Colorado. That's about it."

Elizabeth handed him her empty plate. "The spice factor was pure heaven."

"Cracked pepper. Works magic."

"I'll take two more to go. I'm going to need a bribe."

Cookies nestled in her bag, Elizabeth struck out for her car. Snow dusted the sidewalks, the tips of the lamp poles, and the dozen bronze statues that lined Main. Her favorite was a rhinoceros. Out of place in the western town, the massive statue seemed as surprised as anyone that he was there. A soft white crown looped around his tiny ears, and a stripe of white expanded down his broad back.

A man in a cowboy hat and oiled duster consulted a map near her car. He rotated it first in one direction and then another.

"Excuse me," he said. "Would you be able to point me toward Banner? I got turned around someplace."

Cheeks pockmarked with acne scars framed thin lips. Bushy black eyebrows sprinkled with gray knit together under the brim of his hat. He offered her a smile, his lower teeth a jumble of peaks.

Elizabeth clutched tight to her purse with her elbow. She heard a soft crinkle of protest from the cookie bag. "You aren't too far off. It's only another fourteen miles or so. Follow this road until you pass Stanley Creek and take a right. Easiest way."

The man smiled and extended a leather-gloved hand. "I appreciate this. Not everyone shows kindness to a stranger. You've saved me a lot of time. I'm Tim. Thank you again, uh...?"

In the pause, Elizabeth fought a guttural urge to get in her car and drive off. She chose to give him a half wave instead, and said, "Elizabeth. And it's no problem."

"Indeed." Tim pressed an envelope to her open hand and said, "Elizabeth Blau, you've just been served."

41

"**I**T WASN'T MY FIRST time."

"May it be your last." Charlie tipped back in his tanned leather chair to page through the paperwork she'd been handed.

Tim the Process Server's manilla envelope lay discarded on Charlie's heavy, mahogany desk. Elizabeth's name was printed on a white label. Tim had obscured the envelope with the map. Waited for her to return to her car. Slapped the awful thing into her hand like a brook trout. *She'd been warned not to talk to strangers, hadn't she?*

The confrontation had the lick of violation. Charlie highlighted that it could have happened anywhere. Better on the sidewalk than at work or home. Still, she wanted to wash off the experience, as though she'd found a piece of chewed gum stuck to her shoe.

While Charlie read the filing and took notes, Elizabeth scrutinized his decor.

A man with a home office, he'd spared no expense. An expansive landscape painting hung on the wall behind his desk. Its subject, a paint horse, occupied the foreground and gathering thunderclouds filled the background, their purples in stark contrast to the yellowed grass at the horse's feet.

Shelving covered two walls. Dark, leather-wrapped tomes with gold foil stamping stood at attention between brass bookends. A slew of awards were scattered between the sets of books. Crystal pyramids, black lacquer plaques, and silver figurines traced a life threaded with pro bono cases, charity fundraising, and time spent on nonprofit boards. Several bronze statues rounded out the mood: a bucking bronco, an eagle on a stump, and a pair of baby shoes.

Only one shelf, chest-height, nearest to the desk, said anything other than polished attorney. Crammed with angler magazines, there was color and variety from end to end. Two pictures rested against the spines. In one, Charlie in a rash guard and board shorts, posed on the deck of a ship holding a sizable sea bass out to the camera. In the other, a group of a dozen people in runners' attire held up finisher medals, Charlie among them.

"Well. It's legitimate. Hannah Rae Black claims that Leia—and I'm guessing all other property of Winton Black—is hers, and she wants the dog back. This definitely adds a layer of complexity to Bobby demanding the same."

"Is there any good news, and what will it cost me?"

Charlie held out a hand toward one of the two rust-colored upholstered chairs paired in front of his desk. Elizabeth sat. Charlie pushed a pad of cream paper and a fountain pen in her direction.

"While we wait for the court to sort some things out on their end, we have a little bit of time. If you could outline the costs you've incurred caring for Leia, that would be a start. I'd like to detail how much care was needed to restore her health."

"So there's hope." Elizabeth picked up the pen, felt the weight of its metal barrel.

Charlie propped one ankle up on the opposite knee. "Yes and no. A few cases were settled when the defendant offered to purchase the animal outright. More typical with livestock, though. With household pets, the animal is returned to the original owner, more often than not—if there's proof of that ownership. With a registered dog with more official paperwork than either of us put together, there's likely enough proof."

Elizabeth tossed the pen onto the pad where she'd started with the vet bills. She massaged her temples with both hands. "Waiting on the hope here, Charlie. Tell me something I can work with."

He tapped a finger on a file folder on the desktop. "I wasn't surprised that Hannah came back to claim Winton's estate. To a degree, I wasn't shocked that Bobby would try, either. As business partner and brother, he would have known more about the scope and scale of their holdings than anyone. I was surprised that Hannah's lawyer would have known about one dog out of the many they have. Still have questions about that. Then I found this, and while it only led to more questions, I do have some interesting new information."

Charlie removed a copy of an official document from the folder and handed it to Elizabeth. The sheet was ringed in a decorative edge and included a county seal stamped near the signatures.

"A business license?" Elizabeth studied the paper, forehead crinkled.

The lawyer steepled his hands, patient. "Keep reading."

"...tax registration...sole proprietor of...an animal rescue operation?" Elizabeth reread the license. "I thought he was a breeder."

"It's dated a week before he died. This was a recent venture."

Elizabeth remembered Corbin's comment about Winton having good ideas, his desire to set an example.

"What also stood out to me is that this was an independent venture. Here's the original license for Black Dogs."

Elizabeth scanned the second document he handed over. "Robert Black, Winton Black, and...Hannah Black?"

"Black Dogs sponsored baseball teams, auctions, and the annual fireworks show. Winton attended every event in town, made a point to bring people together. Why he would start a new business without either of his other partners is something I want to know."

"How will this help my case?" Elizabeth thought of the mounting fees.

"Consider this a pro bono situation for the foreseeable future. "Winton had secrets, and I want to know why."

42

"TWICE IN ONE WEEK—HOW does a guy get so lucky?"

Elizabeth found Corbin cleaning out the saloon. He raked old straw into piles which he then scooped up to deposit into a wheelbarrow. The next step was to peel off fresh bedding from a bale to pad each poultry cubby to its nester's liking.

"I wanted to bring Rhett to see Lulabelle. You'd said anytime. But if now doesn't work..."

Rhett tugged on Elizabeth's hand as he reached for every animal. To a two-year old, Burro Buddies was a petting zoo of epic proportions.

"Burb." Rhett pointed at a hen who'd remained in her nest despite Corbin's interventions. Elizabeth gawped at his reaction to the chicken.

"That's Gertie," Corbin said, unaware. He reached up to stroke the wing feathers of the bantam hen. "Stubborn as a mule, but sweet as a rabbit. Would you like to touch her?"

Rhett clasped his hands together as Elizabeth lifted him to the chicken's box. The bird trained one eye on the little boy as small fingers reached for her fluffy underparts. She cocked her head as Corbin guided Rhett's hand along her feathers. Rhett grinned from ear to ear.

"This is the first bird he's been able to touch. Marg's hens run from him. The geese, too."

"Gertie knows a friend when she meets one."

Elizabeth hoped Rhett would repeat his new word. "Where are the rest of them? Rhett adores birds—like everything else."

Corbin pointed toward the back of the building where a door stood open. "I offer sunshine when we get it. Most days they take me up on it. Gertie here is committed to the season. Once she settles in for the long winter, she won't budge."

"I can admire that."

Rhett wandered out onto the porch. "Dog. Dog," he repeated, pointing at the canine lazed out in the weak sunlight.

White eyebrows and muzzle aged the curly-coated retriever sprawled over the deck wood. Rhett knelt to pet her side.

"That's Perdita."

"A rescue?"

He nodded. "And now, an old friend. Found her after a storm, a rope around her neck. Must have broken free from a farm somewhere. She was in bad shape. Fed her up and she became one of the best friends I've ever had. Isn't that the way with good dogs?"

Elizabeth watched Rhett stroke the dog's nose. With a groan, Perdita stretched out to offer her belly up for rubs. "Yeah. I get that."

"Come on," he said. "I've got a llama that's due a hello."

As they meandered through the enclosures, Casey named each animal for Rhett. He detailed their stories, too. Some were lost, others given up, and many were on their way to a new home. They came upon a large corral with multiple troughs and a small barn.

"Donk."

Rhett had ventured a sound at each stop of their tour, and Elizabeth made a mental note of all the new words he said. The appointment with the Billings specialist wasn't until January, but she wanted to catalog all the positive growth she could between now and then.

"Donkeys are how I got started," Corbin said to the little boy. "We call them burros, too. It's how we got our name."

"Bur," said Rhett.

Corbin held up his hand to the boy. "High five, you got it!" Rhett smacked his hand against Corbin's. "We can house up to a dozen burros here. I've got a couple other spots that will work in a pinch, like Lulabelle's. I add spaces as I can afford them."

"Is that how most shelters get started?"

"Many, yeah. Some can build it all at once or do a big remodel down the road. It's all a question of funding. How much you can get and how long it takes you to get a hold of it. I've had a couple of grants, too. Those help. Burros aren't as popular as German shepherds or Persian cats."

They'd come to Lulabelle's cabin. At the sound of their party, the animal stuck her head out the window. Rhett's eyes went wide at the sight of this new animal. He clung to Elizabeth's thigh, his mouth open in a small o. Lulabelle stepped toward the railing. In her winter jacket, she appeared dressed for a formal outing.

"This is a llama, Rhett. LLa-ma." Elizabeth thought of Winton's plans. "Would someone have to have a bunch saved up to get started?"

Corbin slid a wedge of hay into a feeder hooked over the railing. "Feeling sorry for Lulabelle, here? Don't tell me you're switching gears. I know I make it look glamorous and all."

Elizabeth debated what to share. Charlie had suggested she ask Corbin to be a witness should the case with Leia go to trial. Questions might compromise that position. If Charlie's hunch about Winton was right, he may be needed for a different case. She had to ask.

"You said Winton had plans. Good ones. What were they?"

"So, it's not a social call."

Elizabeth bit her lip. "I—"

"Relax. I know you're worried about Leia. I've already told Wolf all I know, which isn't much. Winton came by to get advice. Said we wouldn't be competition as he planned to cater to a special crowd."

"Did he say what kind?"

"No, but I assumed he was giving back."

"How so?"

Corbin removed his hat to scratch at his forehead. He replaced the hat over his shaggy hair. "About a year ago, he had a heart attack when driving a team on the trail. Scary stuff."

"Oh my gosh. What happened?"

"He and Bobby had a couple teams out, exercising. Bobby got to the bottom of the trail, and Winton wasn't behind him.

He left the dogs with the staff, told them to call it in to the sheriff, and took a snowmobile up to search. He met the team coming down the mountain, Winton slumped over the sled."

"How did the dogs know where to go?" Elizabeth recalled the way the mushers stood in the sleds, every muscle in their bodies focused on the teams. Whip in hand, the drivers had every appearance of being key to the sled's direction.

"Likely a combination of instinct and following a trail. That and the lead dogs."

Elizabeth's memory hopscotched through the details of Winton's death. The dog that refused to leave his owner's body at the bottom of the cliff.

"There was no doubt in Winton's mind that without those dogs taking charge, he wouldn't have survived. Said he owed his life to them."

The tags.

43

A SHAGGY FACE LOOMED before Elizabeth before giving her a sound schlep across the face with a warm tongue.

"Max, no! I'm so sorry. He loves everyone. Whether they want him to or not. It's why we're here. Got to teach him to get consent first. Come on, Max, you're coming on too strong!"

Elizabeth wiped at her mouth with the back of her sleeve. All the chairs in the room were filled with people, some with dogs in their laps. Elizabeth took a seat on the floor, cross-legged, at the edge of the group.

Max sat on his hind legs, panting. His owner held his leash taut, so the Irish Setter was forced to maintain his distance. Elizabeth reached out a hand to pat the offender. He nosed at her wrist in response. "It's okay, Max. It's just day one."

The dog's owner reclined against a bulletin board advertising yoga in the park and a dozen business cards for massage therapists. In pressed khakis and loafers with black-framed glasses, they gave off the energy of a closeted superhero, the dog a guise in the pursuit of justice. "I'm Jordan. Cute dog."

"Thanks. I'm Elizabeth, and this is Leia. She doesn't seem sure about this place."

"Jay is a great trainer. He helped Max quit licking his paws. A habit he picked up at the puppy mill, poor thing. You're in good hands."

Leia paced in front of Elizabeth, unsure of the situation. There'd been a sniffing incident with a rambunctious labradoodle and a Yorkie interaction that raised everyone's hackles, but they'd made it through the registration line.

Jo was late. She'd convinced Elizabeth to take the class with her but had yet to arrive.

When she'd first brought up the idea, Elizabeth declined. She didn't want to be seen in public with Leia, give anyone else a chance to sue her for possession of the dog.

Jo argued that working dogs needed a job. Elizabeth thought of the shredded pillows and chewed up sticks at Casey's and reconsidered. Leia loved going to the school, loved being with the kids and the adults. Jo was right. Better to teach a dog how you want them to interact rather than leave it to chance.

Two minutes before the hour, Jo hustled in the door, a golden retriever in tow. "I forgot my notebook," she said. "Wouldn't be able to remember half of what we are supposed to do without it." She handed Elizabeth the leash and extracted the pad of paper and a pen from her hip pack. "I brought treats, too."

"Good. I'm starved."

Jordan chuckled as Max and Jo's dogs sniffed each other.

"Jo, this is Max and his owner Jordan. Jordan, this is Jo and Ranger. Or is it Carly?"

"I brought Ranger today. He's the better listener." Jo stuck out a hand which Jordan shook. "Would you happen to be Jordan Knight, the sports reporter?"

"Depends, are you a fan?"

"Guess I assumed you lived in Billings."

"Many do. Long-time resident of Sheridan, though. Out of curiosity, would you be related to Sheriff Wolf?"

"Depends. Is he coming home late for supper again?"

Jordan laughed. Elizabeth saw the twinkle of braces in the smile.

"He's one of the good ones. Fair. I fact check everything, regardless, but his statements never come up false."

Jo smirked. "So you're saying his offer to bring home Thai takeout for supper tonight is legitimate?"

Before Jordan could reply, a man stood in the front of the room and clapped twice. A square jaw and deep-set eyes gave him the look of a boxer. One arm was wrapped in padding. A pair of gloves poked out of his back pocket, and he wore a whistle around his neck.

"I'm Jay, and this"—he pointed to a cattle dog at his side—this is Tigger."

Tigger kept his eyes on Jay at all times, his snout following the man's gestures.

"I've had Tigger since he was a puppy, and I've trained him to do this." With a whistle and a brief German command, Tigger jumped up to bite hold of Jay's arm. The dog emitted a low, constant growl as it hung in place. Another whistle from the owner and Tigger dropped to all fours.

Every dog in the room watched the interaction, many with hackles on alert. Every human held their breath.

"I also taught him to do this." With a different whistle and another command, Tigger jumped into Jay's arms and licked at his face. "All dogs can be trained. Not all of them can be Tigger, but they don't need to be. We are here to learn how you can work with your dog to provide care. Over the next few weeks, we'll give you the opportunity to get to know your dog. Your dog may be a good fit for hospitals, schools, and nursing homes. At minimum, you'll love each other even more than you do now."

Great, though Elizabeth. *More attachment.*

Jay gave them some basic directions to try and pairs spread out over the linoleum.

"I saw that look."

"What look?"

Jo held out one hand to Ranger. The big golden put his paw in hers and his tongue lolled. She fed him a treat while Leia looked on. Jo passed Elizabeth one of the treats.

"When he talked about attachment. I know you have Rhett on your mind."

Elizabeth held a palm out to Leia who sniffed it, looking for the treat. Elizabeth lifted one of Leia's paws in her open hand, praised the dog, then gave her the treat. "I need a win. I feel like I'm limping along without any concrete answers."

"Speaking of limping, Leia's walk is getting better and better."

"I know. She and Rhett are starting to play together even more. I'm the worst mom ever, Jo. How could I set my son up for his first heartbreak?"

Jay circled the groups, giving tips to some. When he paused before their corner, Jo had Ranger beg and balanced a treat on his nose. Jay applauded the golden and turned to Leia.

"Okay, girl," Elizabeth said to the dog. She squatted and held out her palm. Leia licked her face and sniffed for the treat in the other hand. Elizabeth sighed. "All right, you get one easy one." With Jay watching, she set the treat on Leia's nose, counted to ten in her head, then gave the cue. With a flick of her snout, Leia launched the treat in the air and caught it in her mouth.

"Good. Start with what they know, and go from there. A year from now, you'll be amazed how far you've come," Jay said. He left them to help Jordan with Max.

Elizabeth's heart sank to her gut. "A year from now, all I'll have is a trophy that says Worst Mom of the Year sitting on Casey's mantle."

"What did you learn from Charlie?"

"Not much that's helpful at the moment. He said I could make an offer to buy Leia to settle things. The problem there is that it's not yet clear to whom she belongs."

"Because Bobby says the business is his, Hannah says it's hers, right?" Jo coaxed Ranger to roll over and play dead. "You know, I think Bessie would make a good emotional support animal."

Elizabeth tried to encourage Leia to shake. The buzzing of the fluorescent lights of the recreation room made her head pound. "Don't think Buck would appreciate her being gone all the time.

"Not likely."

Elizabeth tried again to signal Leia with her palm. This time, the dog pawed at her hand. Elizabeth jumped up. "Did you see that?"

44

THEY LINGERED IN THE parking lot after class, allowing the dogs to sniff around the exterior of the building. *Maybe not everyone*, Elizabeth thought.

"Why am I doing this to Rhett? To myself?"

Jo wrapped her arms around her friend and gave her a hug. "Because love isn't something you turn on and off like a light switch. Pets are part of our family."

Elizabeth sagged into her friend's arms. Jo was right.

Jo stepped back, resting her hands on Elizabeth's shoulders. "It's not just about you and Rhett. Think of the kids at school who don't get that love in their lives often, if at all. You'll be giving them something they've been missing."

"Until I have to take it away." Elizabeth opened the passenger door to her car and Leia hopped in. She rounded the back of the car to reach in and start the engine and bring her car to life. With a clunk, the door closed as the heater warmed the inside. On the pavement, Elizabeth stomped her feet to keep blood flowing to her toes. "You asked what Charlie learned. Apparently, Winton was going to make a rescue shelter. For sled dogs. Something about wanting to give back."

Jo pinched her chin. "So that's why he asked me about forming a board of directors. Said he had a really big project on the horizon. One that could involve people from all over the place. I assumed he was joining a nonprofit, not starting one."

The parking lot was empty except for a blue and white pickup truck with an attached camper shell. Jay's Dog Training and a phone number were painted on the side.

"It hasn't missed my attention that the man who died and made it next to impossible for me to adopt a sled dog wanted nothing more than for people to do just that."

"It doesn't help anything now, but he would have been happy to know you are the one caring for Leia. You and Rhett. He liked people who liked dogs."

Jay waved at them as he crossed the lot to his truck with Tigger. When he backed out of his spot, his headlights reflected off the identification hanging from Ranger's collar.

"Clint said Winton wore dog tags. Gold ones. Have you ever seen them?"

"I did. Wore them every day since he left the hospital after the accident."

"Must have been incredible to find yourself alive after all that."

"Ryland was on call that day. Described his survival as a miracle. Everyone was overjoyed by the triumph."

45

T HE DATE HAD BEEN circled in red, a glaring reminder. To-day, Nick would arrive to whisk his son to Seattle for the agreed upon holiday visit. Elizabeth had said yes back in the summer. Back before the reality of this date would have any effect on her life.

It wasn't that she didn't want Nick to see his son, that she didn't understand the difficult decision he'd had to make. His career in architecture needed a place with lots of buildings. Tall buildings, big buildings. She didn't want to live in a city. This compromise was the next best thing.

Or so she told herself.

Over the phone, they'd walked through the pick-up. The introduction of Nick to Leia. Some play time in the yard. A quick goodbye. A pit stop at a Montana emu ranch for distraction. Prayers.

The hope was that Rhett would take it well. That Elizabeth would take it well.

Thus far, she only held out hope for one.

All was going well enough until Nick picked up Rhett and walked toward his car. She'd plastered on her biggest smile and waved to her son. Tears stung at the corner of her eyes and her knees went weak. Still, she waited. Then came the fussing.

"No! No! No!"

Through the rear window she could see Rhett arch his back. Nick struggled to strap him in.

She called through clenched teeth, still smiling. "Need any help?"

From inside the car, Rhett changed tactics. "Dog! Dog!"

As her little boy began to shriek, her nerves wavered. Sweat moistened her brow.

"Nick?"

A giant sob came from the car. Nick gave a triumphant grunt. He stood from his crouched position and closed the car door.

"It's my turn, Liz. Let me be the parent."

"But he's upset. This is new. He needs a chance—"

Nick spun to face her and lowered his tone. "I am trying to believe that you didn't do this on purpose. That you didn't get a dog just so he wouldn't want to see me, but this isn't helping."

"Of course not!" Elizabeth's eyes were wide with shock. He'd thrown the accusation at her like a wet towel.

"Then let me have my time with my son. I'll see you in two weeks." His lips set in a firm line, he got in his vehicle and drove off, the flailing hands still visible in the rear window.

Casey came out of the house, Leia behind him. The dog stood in the driveway, watching the cloud of dust move down the road. She whined in its wake.

"Let's get inside," he said. "I've got Grandma's corn chowder on the stove. I think we could use some comfort."

46

S UNDAY SUPPER AT THE Wolf house was a solemn affair. Jo made a big chef's salad. She argued that no one ate enough greens in the winter. The three of them chewed their roughage in relative silence.

"Enough silence," Jo said. A quarter hour had passed without commentary. "Casey, how's business?"

Casey swallowed a mouthful of butterleaf lettuce and took a big gulp from his water glass. "Decent. Got a small market chain in Denver that's interested in carrying my line. They loved the beer pairings Liz suggested. Said they could market that."

"You'll have products flying off the shelves."

"Looks like I'm going to hire an assistant in the new year. Unless my sister wants to quit the teaching grind to work with me..."

Elizabeth stabbed a hunk of tomato. "You couldn't afford me, and I need health insurance. Give me a year though. I'll save up a bit more. Then we'll talk."

"Brewing is heating up then, I see. Should Clint and I put in for our Super Bowl pony keg now? He'll want an IPA. Too bitter for me. Better also put us down for that stout Casey was going on about. We'll have guests to help."

"Hold up. I haven't had a chance to check into the legalities of selling. I don't want to lose my license before I start."

Casey reached for the bread basket. "That didn't stop the bootleggers. Think of the cool cars we could drive."

Elizabeth threw her napkin at Casey, and Jo laughed. "Just don't give me any details. I need the ability to deny everything."

A knock on the door stopped the mirth. Jo glanced at the wall clock before excusing herself. "Can't imagine what this is. I'll be back in a flash. And save room for banana pudding!"

From the dining room, Elizabeth and Casey heard Jo greet the arrival. "Now Ryland, we were at the table, eating. You know you don't need to knock. Just come in and take a seat." Her voice grew louder as she approached.

Ryland's reply came right behind. "I'm here on business, Jo. Have to follow protocol."

When the deputy met Elizabeth's eyes, his face fell. He removed a stack of papers from under his arm and handed them to her. "Elizabeth Blau, I'm here to seize the rightful property of Hannah Black. Please hand over the Chinook dog by the name of Princess Leia of Alderon."

Jo threw down her napkin. "Ryland, how could you? It's Sunday."

"Seriously?"

Ryland looked to his feet. "I'm sorry, y'all. It's my job."

"Where is that no-good husband of mine? Why isn't he here doing the dirty work?" Jo, protective of Ryland like a son, waffled in her allegiance.

From her seat at the table, Elizabeth spoke up. "It's okay everyone. I've got a plan."

47

THREE AMARETTO SOURS IN and the bartender had his eye on Elizabeth. He kept looking at her over the glasses he wiped as though attempting to assess if now was the time to call for a cab.

She'd glanced at her disheveled appearance in the mirror behind the bar and didn't blame the man. Chestnut locks were plastered to her forehead where she'd rested it in her hands as she stared down at her glass for the last half hour. Torn sweatshirt, ratty jeans, and a smear of mascara down her cheek.

"Tough night?" Alma sidled up to the bar and ordered a lager.

"That stuff tastes like watery lemonade," Elizabeth said.

"Are you an expert on beers?" Alma began to peel the bottle's label between sips.

"Something like that," Elizabeth said.

Alma pushed the bottle aside and ordered a cocktail. "Can I ask why you look like something the cat dragged in?"

Elizabeth grinned from ear to ear. "How long have you got?"

"A vodka soda worth, now" she said.

"Well, in a nutshell, I can't seem to stop losing things in life. I know everything isn't sunshine and roses, but after a while, you start to feel like a punching bag for the universe." Elizabeth nursed her drink. Fingers on the lip of the lowball glass, she spun it in a slow circle through the condensation.

Alma handed her a salt shaker from along the bar and a paper napkin. Elizabeth salted the paper and set her drink on top. "Thanks. I'd forgotten that trick."

"Learned it in my bartending days," Alma said.

"Speaking of employment, would you happen to be the Alma who did an expose on puppy farms last year?

Alma opened her mouth as though to deny it and then gave a little shrug. "You got me."

"So why sled dogs?"

"Dogs get injured or die on the trail all the time, and no one hears about it in the media. It's one thing to keep up tradition, it's another to do it at the sacrifice of animal lives. How did you know?"

"Research," Elizabeth said, and took a swig from her glass.

"Okay then, you know my secret. Tell me one of yours."

Elizabeth's shoulders sank, and she sighed, staring down into her rocks glass. "This is the first time I've been away from my son since he was born. I know it's important for him to spend time with his father as well, but in a selfish way, I feel like I'm getting punished for not being willing to put up with his cheating father."

"That is rough. I'm not a parent, but I'm a kid of divorced parents, and I know the push and pull that comes with that situation."

"And to top it all off, I've lost my own dog."

"Lost? Oh no! I can totally help you. Where did you last see them? Do you want me to make flyers? I'm not from here, but I can staple posters like nobody's business."

"Thanks, but no, it's more complicated than that. I found her abandoned in a doorway and have been fostering her. She is part of a court case now between the business partner and ex-wife of a guy who died."

Alma stared at Elizabeth. "Do you mean Winton Black?"

Elizabeth nodded. "With him gone, everyone seems to want to get their hands on any part of his estate they can."

"Including the animals," Alma said. "Hey. I've got something to show you."

From out of her canvas satchel, Alma pulled out a small tablet. She swiped through some files until she found the right video and pressed play.

"This looks like it's from the Carol Night," Elizabeth said.

"It is."

The video was grainy. Shot from the edges of the room, darkness permeated the edge of the image. In the background, she could see herself talking to Eddie near the palm tree. The camera must have been on one of the cocktail tables that ringed the room.

A voice could be heard off camera.

"Didn't expect to see you back here," the voice said, deep and resonant.

A woman's voice now. "Thank you for the warm welcome."

"I'm guessing you came for what's left of Winton's life."

Fluffy, curly hair filled the screen as the speaker backed into the sight of the camera. "I've got an ironclad claim."

"I wouldn't be too sure. You don't even like dogs."

"I don't have to like them to understand business. You let me worry about —"

There, the recording cut out.

Elizabeth stared at the non-black screen. "Do you have any more footage like this?"

"You betcha. Give me a day or two."

"Alma, this could be the beginning of a legitimate friendship."

48

"YOU ALL ARE OFFICIALLY the worst Christmas company this house has seen since my Aunt Kitty tore through one year with a new tax accountant boyfriend, twenty years her senior. Supper was dead silent, we skipped presents, and my mother drank half a bottle of mint liqueur before throwing up in a potted plant."

"Sounds like a party to me," Casey said. "Sorry I had to bring my mopey sister, it being a family holiday and all."

Elizabeth tossed a throw pillow at Casey's head. He caught it and stuck out his tongue at her.

They were sprawled around Margery Hart's sitting room. Deep bookshelves lined the walls, a ladder providing footing for the highest nooks. Several leather wingback chairs circled the fireplace.

"Anyone care for brandy?" Randall, Margery's assistant, carried a silver tray with a crystal decanter and several matching glasses into the room.

"Yes, please," Elizabeth said.

"Make hers a double," Marg said.

"If you serve it in one glass, a double becomes a single."

Marg crossed to a chair draped with a shawl. She accepted a glass from Randall and spread the fabric over her lap. Randall crouched to tip the fire screen toward himself while he stoked at the burning wood. Sparks flew and spluttered out on the flagstones.

"We've dispatched with the expected frivolity. You now have my ear and it had better be good."

Elizabeth had grown close with Marg over the last few months, since Marg's son Justin had died. Grieving in Justin's absence strengthened their bonds as they navigated the road forward.

Casey swirled the amber liquid in his snifter. "How much brandy have we got?"

"As much as it takes."

Elizabeth unveiled the heartache that had consumed her. She told the tale to the flames burning inside the fireplace, knowing that if she were to see pity on anyone's face, she would burst into tears. When she came to the end of her story, the room was silent in recognition.

Marg tossed the rest of the contents of her glass down her throat. "My dear, that is a lot of gut punches with no recovery time. No wonder you are miserable."

"It could get worse. I could—"

"Tut tut, none of that. We don't want to tempt fate. Instead, how about you suffer through another Hart tradition?"

Casey downed the remainder of his own glass. "Oh, goodie, can't wait. Might need my own double for any more fun we plan to have tonight."

"Randall? Will you bring in the photo albums?"

At this request, a knot formed in Elizabeth's stomach. Would Marg force them to look at dozens of pictures of Justin? She thought of that night with him, the feel of his hand on the small of her back. The way his eyes turned a storm gray when she listened to her. His casket, draped with lilies, being lowered into the ground.

Some people leave an indelible mark, however brief your time together. Justin was one of them.

Casey met Elizabeth's gaze and nudged his chin toward the door. He couldn't be excited to lament over pictures of his longtime roping partner and ex-flame. She shook her head in two quick movements. There was a towering chocolate cake that had yet to be sliced.

Randall returned with two weighty albums in his arms. "Pewter Family from 1952 to 1971."

Marg accepted the books onto her lap. "Thank you, Randall. You leave tomorrow?"

"Bright and early. There's a mai tai on a beach with my name on it."

"Go ahead and get to packing. I can take things from here."

"You sure?"

Exasperated, Marg shooed him away with one hand. "I may be old, but I'm not yet a vegetable. I can slice a cake for my guests."

Randall gave Marg a wry smile, then leaned down to give her a hug. "If you need anything, you know where I work."

"Have a decadent time."

Her assistant dispatched, Marg set the books on the low coffee table, the firelight flickering against the pages as she turned them. Each gave a mute crackle, the plastic sheeting pressed between the pages. An occasional photo would slip free of its confines and drift to the floor.

"Now this is a haircut," Casey said when he returned an escaped picture to its proper placement. In the picture, a boy in a rainbow-striped sweater sat on Santa's lap. His bowl cut meant a halo of hair dusted his eyebrows and the tops of his ears.

"That's my cousin, Dayton. Poor guy. Pinching pennies meant he received the extent of my aunt's beauty school training."

"Who are they?" Casey pointed to a picture of three men standing in a line on a dock, their arms draped over each other's shoulders.

Marg squinted at the photo. "More cousins," she said. "On my mom's side. Rascals, all of them. They'd push me into the water whenever they could."

Elizabeth found herself drawn to the older photos. "Where was this?"

"Lake DeSmet. We'd head down to the spillway or the lake, as far as we could get with what little gas we had, and cool off in the water. My mom always made them take me along. I think she and my aunt just wanted the kids out from underfoot so they could drink and gossip."

Elizabeth pulled the other photo album into her lap. The hefty cover folded back to reveal a young Marg Hart. She wore an embroidered dress with a scalloped collar in one photograph, and a shelf of bangs framed her face. The little girl straddled a bicycle with a banana seat and a teddy bear lounging in the handlebar basket. Elizabeth ran a finger along the edge of the photo.

"I loved that bike," Marg said. As she spoke, her hammered gold earrings caught the firelight. "I thought I could go any-where, be anyone I wanted to be. On my bike, I felt indepen-dent, capable."

Elizabeth thought of Rhett. When would he start riding a bike? Would he want to be gone from dawn until dusk? Her heart ached at the idea. How was it possible she already missed the boy he had yet to become?

"I see that face," Marg said. "Don't insult me by mourning a living son."

It was a sharp rebuke, but a just one.

"You're right." Elizabeth wiped away the tears that threat-ened to fall with the back of her hand. She turned the next page to find a dozen photos of a family camping trip. Adults, tents, and one fluffy cocker spaniel adventured across the images. In one, the kids all stood on a cliff top, hands tented at foreheads, eyes to the horizon like a band of explorers.

"I didn't know you played tennis." Casey stood behind Marg's chair to examine the other album from over her shoul-der.

"All-state champion."

The next page in Elizabeth's book continued the camping adventure. Marg and a brother attempting to make a fire. Her sister hoisting a huge trout on a fishing line, its silver scales winking in the sunlight. A blurry photo of a woman who must be Marg's mother, head tilted back, mouth open wide in a peal of laughter. Near the end of the collection, Elizabeth paused.

"Marg, where is this?"

"Oh, that? It's a lovely little spot at the foot of the Big Horns. We used to go there to pick wildflowers."

Elizabeth continued to stare at the photo, willing a memory to surface. "Tell me about it. Was it popular?"

"I remember it being one of many grassy meadows edged by a stream. At the edge of a ranch lane. Ample sunshine, grasses as far as the eye could see, and space. Just us and nature."

Then it clicked.

"Did it have a name?"

"Lupine Meadow. Or rather, that's what we called it. In the books, I think it's named after the creek."

"Any chance you could recognize the place now?"

"Pretty sure I could, why?"

Elizabeth set the book on the table. "I've got a call to make."

49

I N RICKETY HEELS, ELIZABETH made a beeline for her target.
Snagging an invitation to the Musher's Gala had been
the first step. Gary, as a competitor, was all too happy to have
her as his plus one for the night. Drivers received gratis tickets
for the meet-and-greet. The fundraiser was sponsored by the
Big Horn Cultural Association, and non-drivers used it as a
chance to trot out their wealth in the name of a good cause.

Jo warned her the party was an excuse for the richest county
residents to get together and gossip, but Elizabeth was determined to be in attendance. There was someone she needed
to see.

The tables were draped in a navy, satin tablecloth. Silver
snowflake confetti lined the buffet tables covered in charcuterie and fondue offerings. A life-sized ice sculpture of a
husky was the centerpiece of the dessert table. The dog was
surrounded by dozens of white and blue Petit fours and mini
cheesecakes.

A three-piece band commanded the stage. A few couples
danced while all the rest of the guests mingled.

Elizabeth had left Gary at the coat check. He'd been all too
happy to have her volunteer to be his designated driver. When
they arrived, he saluted her and headed for the bar.

Hannah Black held court at a banquet table. Martini glass
in hand, her attention was on her dining companion. The man
would say a few sentences to her under his breath. Hannah
would pat him on the shoulder or on his thigh and throw her

head back to laugh, as if nothing funnier had ever been said before.

Hannah Black, her target.

A few feet away from the woman, Elizabeth hesitated. She didn't have a copy of the video to prove what she'd heard. What if the conversation backfired? *Careful, Liz.*

Elizabeth approached the couple and hovered a few feet away. The man nudged Hannah with his elbow and pointed to Elizabeth.

Hello," said Hannah. "We're fine on drinks, thanks."

Elizabeth looked down at the plain black dress she'd donned for the event. Caterer hadn't been her goal for the look. "My name is Elizabeth Blau. You had the Sheriff take the best friend my son has ever had away from us. She's in one of your cold kennels somewhere instead of warm inside our house with a family that loves her. I wanted to talk to you in person in case there's any chance you would change your mind about her."

Confusion crossed Hannah's face. Her eyebrows drew together as she seemed to try to connect Elizabeth's story with her arrival at the event.

Her companion pushed back his chair and stood up. "Sounds like you have some business to discuss. I'm going to circulate. Let me know when you're...free."

Hannah sent him a beaming smile. He nodded at Elizabeth and wandered off to join others deep in discussion about their golf club memberships and winter chalets.

Before Elizabeth could renew her inquiry, Hannah whispered at her through gritted teeth. "Do you have any idea who that was? You might have just cost me a date with a cattle baron. If you have an issue with my lawyers, I suggest you talk to them."

Hannah looked around the room, as though assessing on whom to prey next.

"Look," Elizabeth said. "I'm just hoping you'll take pity on me as a mother and let me work something out with you about the dog."

"The dog? You interrupted me to talk about dogs." Hannah's eyes flashed, dangerous, as though a lioness, considering a pounce.

"I'd be happy to buy her from you, and then we can be done with this. Then I won't have to interrupt you ever again."

Hannah stood up and tucked a clutch under her arm. "Look, I don't know who you are, but if this has anything to do with Winton's estate, you can go through my lawyers. That's my family's land we're talking about. I am not letting business technicalities screw me out of anything I deserve. He was already trying to throw it all away on charity when he was alive, and I'm sure not letting him do it from the grave."

At this pronouncement, she stormed off. Elizabeth didn't dare to follow.

From Elizabeth's left, Gary handed her a champagne flute and took the now empty seat. He plucked one of the silvery snowflakes from the tablecloth and held it up to the light. "So, that went well."

"It didn't solve my problem, but I'm pretty sure she didn't kill Winton."

"How do you know that?"

Elizabeth tipped the flute back, and the tiny bubbles poured down her throat. Finished, she smacked her lips together.

"Because she's telling the truth about the legal hassle. In Wyoming, if you die, your estate goes to your spouse if you don't have kids. The presence of lawyers means it's not a simple situation, so why throw a murder into the mix?"

"Well, if she's innocent, then who isn't?"

"That is exactly what I need to find out."

50

A FTER THE FLUTE OF champagne, Elizabeth chugged a couple glasses of water. She needed to be in the clear before giving Gary a ride home.

Her companion rested one elbow on the corner of the bar, a highball glass in hand. He'd unbuttoned his suit coat and was talking to a man Elizabeth recognized from the bank. *Go Gary*, she thought.

She wandered over to the food tables to snag a few charcuterie skewers. Napkin in hand, she stepped over to the window to look out across the lawn. Prosciutto wrapped mozzarella balls made for a good snack while she tried to think.

The scent of cedar and bergamot preceded a voice in Elizabeth's ear. "I recommend the stuffed dates."

"Eddie." Elizabeth couldn't hide her smile. "I didn't think you were still here."

"I wasn't. Or rather, I had to come back and close out some business."

"The last payment."

"Something like that. I've got an investment and I plan to see it through."

"Sounds ominous." Elizabeth popped an olive into her mouth.

Eddie laughed. "Let's just say I want to finish what was started. Go out with a bang, you know?"

The scattered city lights outside the windows reflected in his eyes. He smirked, as if to an inside joke, and took a sip of his drink.

Like a cat with a mouse in sight. Did Eddie have something to do with Winton's death?

A man in a tuxedo stepped to the microphone stand on a small stage at the front of the room. He tapped the mic twice. Muffled sounds echoed across the room as the guests quieted their chatter.

"Good evening, everyone. Thank you all for coming." Here, he paused and waited for silence. "Before we get to the live auction part of our evening, we have a very special award to bestow and a guest of honor who will be saying a few words on behalf of the recipient."

Applause scattered around the room like snowfall.

Eddie twisted his lips into a sneer. "This is my cue to exit."

"Not one for speeches?"

"My family hasn't put up with lip service from the Black family for decades. I'm not about to break that tradition tonight. If you'll excuse me." With a gentle touch on her shoulder, he was gone.

51

E DDIE'S BACK STRAINED AT the seams of his tailored suit, all muscle and sinew. The man was attractive, alluring, and smelled like a night you'd give anything to relive. It was more than that, though. Within his eyes were several lifetimes across continents, the kind of history you needed to know. Here was a man whose story ran deep, a pool into which she wanted to fall.

Hate to watch them go, love to watch them leave.

He threaded his way through the guests to exit out the front door. A half step behind him, Hannah Black followed. Elizabeth choked on a stuffed date.

She reached for a cocktail napkin to cover her face while she gagged on the almond that had wedged itself somewhere in her esophagus. A nearby couple gave her worried looks as she hacked like a cat with a hairball.

The woman bent to peer at Elizabeth, who'd doubled over. "Are you okay?"

"Perhaps we should do the Heimlich," the man said to the woman. He then shouted at Elizabeth as though the problem were with her hearing. "Should we do the Heimlich on you?"

Elizabeth wanted to laugh but worried that would do her in. She wheezed and spat until the bulk of the date was wadded into the napkin in her hand. After a few deep breaths, she turned to face the concerned couple.

"You know, each year, around five thousand people die from choking." She deposited the napkin in a discrete trash can underneath the buffet table and left in search of a club soda. The couple stared after her, mouths agape.

The bartender, a scrawny man with a slim mustache and rolled sleeves, was only too happy to serve her a fizzy water topped with a lime wedge. Elizabeth imagined what her face must look like, post-choking. Red and puffy, eyes watery.

Glass in hand, she skirted the room to find an empty chair in proximity to the door. She would stick around to see when Hannah—or Eddie—returned.

Seated, Elizabeth tuned into what was happening on stage. Bobby Black was handed a plaque by the emcee. Black wrapped it in his arms as though it were a teddy bear. The emcee explained that Winton was to be recognized as someone who'd contributed to the cultural significance of the county through the historic sport of sled dog racing.

"Speech!"

"Yes, speech!"

Shouts came from the crowd who held glasses aloft to the proposed speaker.

"Mr. Robert Black will now say a few words about his brother."

The men on stage hugged again before Black stepped to the microphone. He looked down at the plaque and then out to the audience, as if he couldn't believe the evening was real.

Black's jacket shone with the cheap satin of an off-the-rack purchase. He'd paired it with dark denim jeans and black boots. The boots were polished, though, and his hair tamed into slick waves behind his ears. Elizabeth would bet that the shirt beneath the coat had the well-known Black Dogs emblem embroidered over the pocket. Maybe even his socks. She was surprised the Band Aid on his hand didn't also have the company logo plastered across its surface.

"Good evening, everyone. Thank you so much for hosting us for the fifth year in a row as we come together to celebrate the sport of sled dog racing. This is the first year my brother won't be by my side, coaching me to the finish line."

Bobby emitted what would qualify as a dignified sob into his sleeve. *Maybe an inexpensive coat was a strategic move*, Elizabeth thought. Still no sign of Eddie or Hannah.

"For over four decades, we've been a team. I've lost more than a fellow musher and business partner. I lost my best friend, my brother. Our sport lost a giant in Winton Black."

Here, the audience clapped a rousing acknowledgement.

Black gave a great heave of his chest as a tear slipped alongside his nose. His face turned to steel, and he leaned toward the microphone. "That is why I dedicate my race tomorrow, my win for Black Dogs, to my departed brother, Winton Black. I love you, man." He kissed the plaque and made for the steps to exit the stage. A dozen people patted him on the back as he made his way back into the audience.

To her surprise, Elizabeth spotted Hannah near the back of the room. Elizabeth had missed her entry. The woman wasn't clapping. A scowl marred her otherwise beautiful face. She made no effort to hide the disdain palpable to Elizabeth from all the way across the room.

Whatever had been between Bobby and Hannah at one time was no longer familial.

52

R ACE DAY DAWNED COLD and crisp. An overnight snow dump covered the landscape. Everything the sun touched sparkled, the tiny ice crystals like diamonds scattered over the hills.

Jo collected Elizabeth at a painfully early hour to head up the mountain to the ski resort. "Clint went up an hour ago. The race will be half over by the time we get there."

Elizabeth grumbled into her coffee and zipped her jacket up to her chin. "Then we'll be early for next year."

"Hah! Are you always this funny in the mornings?"

"The Iditarod doesn't start until the respectable hour of 10 a.m."

Jo cranked up the heat in her SUV. The tan leather dash, rubbed smooth with time, rattled as the machinery kicked into higher gear. "Alaskans have an altogether different relationship with time."

"It's only three in the morning in Juneau."

"And not a single Alaskan is doing anything about it. There are scones in that bag by your feet. Cram one in your mouth. Cranberry-orange. It'll turn you pleasant."

"Why did I say I would come to this again?"

Elizabeth was only half awake. She'd dragged Gary out of the event when the bar shut down and poured him onto his front door mat. He'd scored the banker's phone number and had celebrated with a fourth scotch.

The whole drive back to her house, Elizabeth had turned over the details of the Black Family drama in her mind, desperate to find a kernel of hope for the return of Leia.

Hannah had made her position clear. Elizabeth would update Charlie about what was said, but he wouldn't be surprised. He'd warned her to let the system do the work.

Elizabeth may be brave, but she wasn't stupid. She didn't think her confidence could take another shut down.

The odds stacked against her like snow on the tree branches. She was bending for now, but it wouldn't be long before she snapped under the pressure. The campaign to reunite her family slipped between her fingers like sand.

"Hey, there, where'd you go just now?"

Elizabeth had stared out the window at the blurred landscape for so long she'd forgotten she wasn't alone. She sat up in the seat and rummaged in the sack to withdraw a scone. It smelled of cardamom and had a sprinkling of sugar crusting its top.

"Sorry 'bout that. I'm not feeling much like myself. These smell amazing, though. Thank you. Maybe I just need some calories."

"What the doctor ordered."

The miles rolled over in the odometer. Along the route, the state had placed signs in front of various rock formations to remind visitors that Wyoming is an ancient place. These mountain sides had stood for millions of years, far longer than the people who inhabited the area now.

"Do you ever think about how much easier life had to be for our ancestors in some ways? They didn't have half the stressors we do. Cars, technology, ex-husbands." Elizabeth spoke her words to the window. Her breath fogged the glass. "Life was easier when there wasn't all this push and pull and climb."

"Was it, though?" Jo watched the road, her gloved hands at ten and two. "Sure, they had fewer complications in their lives, but it was a lot easier to die back then. No grocery stores. And don't tell me you'd rather stay married to Nick?"

Elizabeth plucked a crumb from her shirt. She cracked the window to push it outside. The breath of frigid air whipped around her face until she rolled the glass back in place. "You're right. Sorry, Jo, I'm miserable company this morning, and I know it."

"You're a mom who is doing everything she can to do right by her kid, and that's exhausting. No need to apologize to me."

53

A T THE SKI RESORT, the parking lot was crammed with all-wheel drive cars, trucks, and trailers. It reminded Elizabeth of the parade day. Here, the heavy vehicles were an expected part of the scenery. In addition to dogs and sleds, people backed ski mobiles out of toy haulers while others strapped on cross-country skis. Elizabeth wished she'd brought her snowshoes. Her boots found purchase on the walkways around the starting area, but she wouldn't risk the deeper drifts.

She and Jo made their way to the tented area for officials. Drivers and a dog or two waited in line for information, racing packets, or a chance to warm up by the propane heater. A scouting troop served cookies and hot beverages from a table, and Elizabeth purchased a cup of cocoa.

Clint was parked behind a table reviewing endless documents covered in tiny print.

"Hello, husband. Don't let us interrupt, but we're here. Need anything?"

The sheriff removed his reading glasses and glanced at his watch. "Actually, yes. I need to stretch. Been sitting and reading through vet papers for twenty minutes too long."

Jo handed him a thermos, and they headed to a fire pit where a few spectators stood, warming their hands. A few idle snowflakes caught in Clint's mustache, and he brushed them off.

"Any news?"

Clint removed a scone from the bag. He stuffed half the triangle into his mouth and followed that with some coffee. "These are heaven."

"That's not news," Elizabeth said. "The fact that I didn't eat the whole sack in the car is what should go on the front page. You ought to sell these puppies at Beans."

"Normally, I'd love pure adoration, but it's cold, the clock is ticking, and I have to drive home with this sop of a woman who is desperate for something that will help."

"What happened on that car ride?"

Elizabeth sighed. "It's just where my head is at. Charlie told me that we won't be able to gain more ground in getting Leia back until Winton's estate is settled. It sounds like the courts will be faster about that once the murder investigation is done."

"Ah. Got it. Well, all I can share—which is about all we know at this point—is that the autopsy came back. He died from the fall. It snapped his spine."

"Poor man!"

"No other injuries?"

"Nothing. Winton Black was hale and hearty—until he wasn't."

54

THE DAY DAWNED CLEAR and cold. Fresh powder blanketed the slopes, and the air was so dry it crackled. A frigid wind whipped around the trees, brushed snow off the branches and into the air. Cheeks were pink from the weather of a Wyoming winter morning.

Elizabeth swam through the sea of race-goers, mushers, dog handlers, and spectators gathered on the mountaintop. Waves of brightly colored ski jackets undulated across the gathering. Hot pink, navy blue, and camo-patterned gear were accessorized with beanies, ski goggles, and a rainbow of scarves.

She had to think. Here, among the many faces and voices, she was just one person who was running out of time.

Someone in the crowd would have seen a woman in an orange coat and a chunky-knit scarf wrapped up to her chin. A stranger who scanned the crowd for her family. Her friends. A spectator there to cheer on the teams. Someone who faded into the masses.

Elizabeth snagged a seat on top of a log to think. A few felled trees had been dragged in a semi-circle around the bonfire. Couples and groups huddled near the flames pit to analyze the entrants and keep their fingertips from going numb.

"Length of the race determines their start time. You'll hear the different starts soon."

"My money's on that outfit out of Fairbanks. Have you seen the look of those dogs? They're twice as big as the others. Wolf-sized!"

Two people stamped their feet and gabbed while they balanced cups of coffee in hand. Steam vaporized from the hot contents. Elizabeth could smell the comfort from across the circle.

"Twenty bucks says they don't touch Black." The man held up his cup in a gloved hand to mark the bet.

Orange snow bib smirked into his drink. "He's distracted. Too much pressure riding on today. Fifty bucks on Juneau."

"You're on."

The two moved off to check out the dogs. Others took their seats. Elizabeth stared into the flames as she considered how all the pieces could fit together into anything other than her losing Leia for good. It was as if the ocean of people swirled around her as she sat on the log, chin in hand, wishing reality were something other than the truth laid out before her.

"Shame Winton isn't here. He loved race day. Said the dogs were born for it. There was nothing better than watching them tear out across a trail."

Voices can bring recognition like wildfire. Elizabeth recognized the latest person to join the group by the husky tone and the dismissive air, as though the speaker read from a script she couldn't wait to finish and toss in the trash.

Hannah Black, decked out in a fuchsia snowsuit and dove gray boots, straddled the log next to Elizabeth. With her front teeth, she tugged on each fingertip of one glove to loosen it, then pulled it all the way off. One hand free, she removed the other glove and set both in her lap. Palms out to the flames, she was focused on the fire and not who listened nearby.

"Really?" Her companion was decked out in black, a faux fur lined collar and a dozen silver snaps for embellishment.

"Yep. He used to say that watching nature play out was a privilege. Gave you a real sense of purpose."

Out of the corner of her eye, Elizabeth watched Hannah withdraw a flask from the recesses of her coat, take a swig, and pass it to her companion. Elizabeth was thankful for her oversized hat, sunglasses, and thick neck wrap. There was little of her face visible to be recognized.

The other woman smirked when she accepted the flask. "I see you aren't wearing the family crest."

Hannah looked down at her outfit and scoffed. "Hah. I never wanted to get into the business to begin with. It's a sure bet, he said. We will make our money back, and then some, he said. We just had to find a unique stock of dogs. Offer something no one else had out here."

"He wasn't wrong there. Find me anyone else who has Chinook dogs."

"He was right about the money part. He was wrong, though, about how easy it would be. Nothing in this business is easy. These dogs work hard and play hard which means their keepers do, too. Too hard. I'm looking forward to selling the whole lot to the highest bidder."

Elizabeth gasped. An icy hand wrapped around her heart and squeezed. *Would Leia be sold off as part of a package deal?* Her poor, sweet Leia handed off to who-knows-who to be taken who-knows-where. Panic constricted Elizabeth's throat, and she struggled to take full breaths. She had to do something. Now.

Alma and Ian moved toward Elizabeth. Ian carried the camera on a tripod, an easy giveaway to their location among the masses. They made a beeline for Hannah.

The documentary maker approached Hannah and introduced herself. "Could I ask you a few questions?" Alma waved Ian up as she talked.

"You can ask. I may not answer." Hannah tucked the flask away in her jacket. She fluffed her hair and brushed it back away from her face

With a nod from Ian, Alma began her prompt. "You've made significant profits from raising sled dogs. Some people find this whole thing barbaric. They think the risk of injury to the dogs isn't worth the sport. Any comments?"

"Businesses exist to make profits. I won't apologize for that basic fact," Hannah said. Her eyes went dark. "But I will say that Winton came home injured more often than any dog. Dogs communicate differently than people do. They don't have words, so they have to use their size, their paws, their bark, and sometimes their bite to make a point."

Bite.

Elizabeth dropped her cocoa. When she reached to grab for the now empty cup, she bumped heads with Hannah. The woman had bent to retrieve the trash that rolled her way before the wind took it out across the snow.

Hannah held the crushed vessel out to Elizabeth. "Bad luck there. You okay? You have one seriously hard head." A flash of recognition crossed Hannah's face as she scrutinized Elizabeth.

Elizabeth knew she had seconds to escape. "Good thing only a quarter of people ever experience a concussion. Sorry. I mean, excuse me. I see someone I know. Over there."

Before Hannah could reply or Alma could follow, Elizabeth was nothing more than footprints in the snow.

55

D ESPITE THE COLD, ELIZABETH'S long underwear clung to her skin with sweat. She clenched and unclenched her fists, willing a pathway to surface.

One step toward the starting line, she second-guessed her impulse and turned back. She had to find him. Find her.

Elizabeth checked her watch. There was time, but not much. She had minutes to alter a course that could keep her from Leia forever.

In a circle of people huddled near a large black minivan, Elizabeth spotted him. He was reviewing strategy with the crew, talking dogs, and checking equipment.

Bobby Black had his arms crossed, his head bowed. He listened to one of the race officials, a man in a vest marked Veterinarian. The vet held a clipboard which they tapped with a pen as they detailed an explanation.

Elizabeth tapped a foot, then shifted her weight from one hip to the other while she waited for an audience with Black. When the official finished detailing the paperwork and left, the others followed. Only Black stayed behind. He turned to shoot her an icy glare.

"Can I *help* you?" Black slid sunglasses in place and re-trieved gloves and a pack from inside his van before he slid the door shut with a clunk.

"You can if you choose to. I just want my dog back."

"*Your* dog?" He emphasized *your* as though it were laugh-able, a joke she said to garner a laugh in an otherwise serious transaction. He chuckled as he slipped each glove over his hands, tied a bandana around his neck. "You should double check how ownership works. My purchases, the animals that are part of my business, are mine to do with as I like. I certainly don't owe them to you or anyone else."

"Anyone else meaning Hannah? Or do you mean someone like your brother who wanted to fund a shelter? I'm just trying to understand which excuse you'll use to defend keeping Leia when you don't give a damn about her."

"You don't know the first thing about what I care about." Black clenched his teeth and looked to his left and right.

Before she could spit out a retort, Black wrapped one hand around her throat and shoved her against the van door. No one could see the backside of the van as people pressed toward the starting line.

Elizabeth struggled to speak, any sound impossible to choke out. His gloved hands held her so the cold metal pressed beneath her jacket. Elizabeth twisted, aimed a kick that didn't land.

"Listen, I don't know who you think you are, and I don't care." Black spoke inches from Elizabeth's face. His words shook with emotion, his spittle hitting her cheeks. "I will *not* let anyone get in between me and the success of my business. Do you hear me? I will do what it takes to secure what is mine, and I want that perfectly clear. Now get out of my way. I have a race to win."

Black released Elizabeth, and she fell to the ground, coughing. She grabbed at the fabric around her neck and tossed the scarf to the ground, desperate for air.

Fight had backfired. Flight meant she had to find Clint. Jo. Tell them all she knew. The clock was ticking.

A hand squeezed her shoulder just as her eyes began to refocus on her surroundings, and she jumped.

"We saw it all. More importantly, Ian got it on video."

56

A LMA HELPED ELIZABETH TO her feet. "You okay?"

"You mean, have I gathered myself back together enough to freak right out at you for not stopping him from choking me half to death?" Elizabeth's breath began to slow. She pressed a hand to her chest, assured herself her heart still beat within.

Alma shook her head. "We just finished up with a handler from the Juneau crew. Y'all were in the backdrop. Ian saw Black with his hands on you, kept the camera running, and we ran over."

"Thank you," Elizabeth said to Ian. Elizabeth struggled to tie thoughts together, as oxygen flooded back to her brain. She felt around her neck, her own touch gentle in comparison to Black's fingers squeezing her throat.

"There aren't any marks," Alma said. "Even if you don't bruise, we have evidence. What do we do next?"

"Do you think the video is good enough to get a close-up of his hands? Before he put on the gloves."

Alma looked to Ian, who nodded. Alma said, "It's likely. We were running, so things might be shaky. We need to get it up on a big screen. See what we can do."

"I've got to get the sheriff's attention. Can you help me stall the race?"

"I think we have just the thing."

Elizabeth dove through the hundreds of people gathered on the mountain side. She ducked between lawn chairs and coolers, the entrapments of a tailgate party. Portable propane heaters balanced on snow-packed surfaces. Some spectators flipped burgers, others turned skewers. A few had speakers. To them, this was a festive event. To Elizabeth, it was a reckoning.

Beyond the spectators stood a different crowd. This area was for the racing team, whether mushers at the helm of a sled, team managers, and the slew of dog support personnel. There were nutritionists, massage therapists, acupuncturists, and every other manner of advantage that could be given to an animal's physical fitness. This group was serious, focused. Ready.

Clint was parked under his tent with a clear view of the starting line ahead. The group of yellow vested people consulted each other around him.

Elizabeth was stuck behind the teams as they sorted themselves out onto the starting area. She jumped up and waved both hands to get his attention over the dozens of heads.

He didn't see her among the masses. Another official tugged him toward the starting line and handed him a timer.

The professionals shifted their attention. Sleds lined up, drivers in place, while others followed behind with medical kits, walkie-talkies, and a competitive edge.

Alma and Ian raced for the front of the line and threaded their way through the sleds toward Black.

A monotone mumble over the erected speaker system announced that the race would start in five minutes.

Elizabeth pushed past a father with a child on his shoulders, a group of women wearing matching blue hats. She mounted a three stepped box parked at the edge of the official's booth. The box would hold the winners, hours from now.

From atop this new vantage point, she spotted Alma and Ian.

The reporter held her phone out in front of Black. The man's eyes were glued to her screen. As he watched, the knuckles holding his reins whitened as his face flushed beet red. Ian, a few paces behind, recorded the interaction.

Black wrenched the device from Alma's grip. He threw her phone to the ground and stepped on it with the heel of his boot, crushing the screen into glass shards.

Gary, installed in his own sled behind Black's team, witnessed the altercation. He called out to Black, who yelled back at him. Elizabeth couldn't tell what was said, but Gary waved in the direction of the vested officials.

Black rushed over to his competitor's rig and slugged the driver before he kicked the two closest dogs in the gut. The dogs yelped and ran. Dogs shot in all directions as the entanglement snarled Gary's team. Alma went down in a tangle of straps. A ripple effect of knotted rigging and barking dogs shot through the competitors.

In the ensuing chaos, Black jumped back into his own sled and took up the reins. With a crack of his whip, he took off down the trail.

57

E LIZABETH FOUGHT THROUGH THE melee to Alma. The woman was helping Gary to his feet. Dog handlers spread out between the teams in a bid to untangle the packs. The crowd drew closer to become a physical barricade and help with dog containment. Gary brushed off his snowbib and reseated his hat.

"Are you okay?"

"He's getting away!" Alma took hold of Elizabeth's sleeve and pointed the way to Black's retreat.

Elizabeth squinted against the bright sunlight. She took in the crowd, dogs, and people everywhere. Loads had been tossed over, gear strewn over the icy surface, gloves and hats trampled. This would take forever to sort out. "I'm going after him," Elizabeth said. Before Alma could protest, she doled out orders to the woman. "Find the sheriff and tell him what happened and where I went. I'll stay back on the trail, but I've got to keep him in sight. We can't let him get away."

Near the trailers sat the emergency response team's snowmobile, key in the ignition. Elizabeth hopped on and pushed the start button. The machine roared to life, and she squeezed the throttle. It shot forward from underneath her, and Elizabeth almost slipped right off the back.

There wasn't time for a lesson. With a quick prayer, she tried a second time. The machine took off. This time, Elizabeth clung to the seat with her thighs, eyes focused on the trail ahead.

Black, in full, branded gear, was easy to spot against the snow white landscape.

Elizabeth kept her distance. She had a tentative grip on the snowmobile and wouldn't risk a flip. Colored markers stapled to trees indicated the trail. She didn't dare cut across anything that wasn't a trail. Still, responsive turns and a greater potential for speed allowed her to catch up to her target.

Like a snake, his team whipped around curves. The shout of his voice echoed through the canyon as he demanded the dogs go faster. At one point, he looked back, eyes wild, with his nostrils flared at her pursuit.

Switchbacks striped the mountainside like lashes from a whip. Ponderosa pines edged the next curve, a defensive line. Black drove his team on approach—faster, relentless.

Elizabeth braked, unsure of navigating the serpentine, cliff-side trail, and began to fishtail. The rockface loomed on one side as the snowmobile bucked and fought control. Snow flew off the edge, along with rocks and branches that tumbled behind.

As the back of the machine skidded left, she eased off the gas and turned the handlebars into the slide. Her knuckles ached from the grip. She held tight until the tracks evened out and she sailed forward once again.

Just keep him in sight, that's all.

She could do this.

She would do this.

58

T HE MOUNTAIN LOOMED, STEEP and forbidding. Elizabeth focused forward. If she watched the trail in front of her, she could balance speed and agility. Two more turns and she was again at an open stretch. No sign of Black. She slowed the engine to a purr and listened.

White blanketed the foreground. The lack of color blurred the surface, trees the only detail. Snow stretched out for acres ahead. A canvas of nothing.

A flash of motion and color signaled from behind a copse of lodge poles. Elizabeth eased the ride forward.

She zipped across two hundred yards to meet the trees. Black had veered off course and over a hill. The rise hid the small ravine.

The yelps and snaps of the sled dogs were the first sounds she heard. As she approached, slow and cautious, human moans floated over the din of dogs.

Elizabeth stopped the vehicle and dismounted. Her heavy breath puffed clouds of moisture into the cold, dry air. For a moment, she fumbled in her pocket for her multi-tool. With a flick, the tiny knife shot out, winking in the sunlight. A small security against whatever lay ahead.

Each footstep through the drifts was a chore as she slogged through the snow.

With tentative balance, she eased down the bank. The dogs pulled at their ties but appeared to be otherwise unharmed. A few leapt and lunged when they saw her, barking.

Black was pinned under a flipped sled. He was stuck under the sled's angled surface, his bulk down in a tree well. Bindings were knotted, twisted, one leg at a scary angle.

A flutter at Black's throat. A cough.

"Help is coming," Elizabeth said, unsure if it was true. She set one cautious foot in front of the other as she approached the scene of the crash. Black was unlikely to rise and attack. Still, she kept her distance. "Can you hear me?"

Black moaned again. He turned his head toward the sound of her voice. His eyes blinked once, twice, and again. He spat flecks of blood onto the snow. "Go to hell."

Elizabeth sucked in her lips and gave a slow nod. "Yep. You're good for now." She turned to address the pack.

She arranged harnesses and leads with careful attention to each dog's position and ability to contribute. Elizabeth mapped out the straps. Plan in place, she made a few, deft cuts with her tiny knife.

One strand of dogs came free. She anchored that set around the nearest trunk, knotting the end of the leather. The second line was easier. In minutes, the dogs were sorted. Some panted, reclined. Others waited upright, shifting weight from paw to paw. Elizabeth cataloged their personalities. How would Leia fit in?

She called over to Black. "It didn't have to be this way. I just wanted my dog."

"And Winton just wanted to volunteer." Black coughed and swore.

"That's what I don't get." Elizabeth, satisfied the dogs were sorted, returned to sit on the snowmobile. She looked toward the trail—nothing yet—then looked back at Black. "What would it hurt to run a shelter on the side?"

"Only the entire business that made it possible for him to sit around and become a damned do-gooder. The business I put my blood, sweat, and tears into so we could have that success. Become champions. Make money. He had no issue throwing away all of my hard work because he had some near-death experience. It's easy to be a giver when you don't have to pay. My brother was never the head of the business. I always had to keep us above water, and just when things were going well, he wanted to throw it all away. A shelter would have drained every ounce of profit we'd made. That's what." Black shifted a shoulder. Pain wrenched his face.

"It was the hand that gave you away, you know."

Black grunted and spat again. "What are you talking about?"

"Brutus bit you, that day. Didn't he?"

A beat of silence. Then a growl. "That damn dog should be put down." One of the sled dogs whined, ears perked. A few others got to their feet. "The other one, too."

"What did Leia ever do to you?"

There were two dog tags. At first, Elizabeth assumed they were military style. Two of the same tag, one chain. But sleds ran with pairs of dogs. Brutus and Leia were team leads.

"It's more what my brother did for them. All because he didn't die on the mountain top."

"You kicked her out of the van at the race, didn't you? Hurt her and left her in the street to die."

Black winced when he tried to shift his position. He panted, his face sweating from the effort despite the frigid conditions. "My brother was distracted. I needed her out of the way."

"Having a big heart shouldn't cost a life."

"Winton chose his path. I chose mine."

A deep rattle sounded up the mountainside. The noses of three other snowmobiles crested the hill. The dogs shifted in the drift, anxious. Elizabeth waved her hat in the air, a bright flag. Each machine turned her way.

In the tent, the crinkle of the emergency blanket did little for Elizabeth. Black's cold-hearted deeds chilled her to the bone, and she was shaking at his heartless actions.

"And that's all he said?"

"Yeah." A shudder followed her sentence. "Is he going to make it?"

"Black? Yeah. His leg is twisted up something nasty, but it sounds like he'll live to face consequences."

Elizabeth nodded. "Good."

"Anything else come to mind?"

The last hour was a flurry of activity that played in front of Elizabeth like a silent movie. The snowmobiles carried the sheriff and others from the race. They'd radioed for a helicopter. Packed her onto the back of one of the vehicles. Tended to the dogs. To Black.

She'd found herself in the plastic chair, wrapped to her ears, a hot coffee pressed into her grip. Authorities buzzed around her. A light shone in her eye, a face loomed behind it. Her temperature was checked. Her pulse. She waited for the buzzing to stop, for the world to cease to spin.

The helicopter left with Black inside before she was loaded onto a snowmobile behind the sheriff.

Now Clint Wolf, sheriff and friend, waited. Patient.

"No. That's it."

He set a light hand on her shoulder, a wrinkle in the shiny, silver foil. "If you think of anything, just say the word."

Elizabeth spotted Jo, on her way to the tent. "You know I will."

59

ELIZABETH SQUATTED AMONG THE piles of laundry. All socks had been paired save a single, small green sock covered in crocodiles. Rhett's. For a moment, she let herself cling to the single sock, holding it to her cheek and missing her son, before she continued her hunt for its mate.

At her insistence, Casey had left. He'd hovered over her all morning. Offered coffee. An omelet. Ibuprofen. Whisky. She'd shooed him away when the attention overwhelmed her and sought relief in a mundane chore.

In a purple, plastic basket, the missing sock appeared, stuck in the cuff of a pant leg.

Elizabeth held it up. "Aha!" The sound of her voice broke the silence. "That's how it starts, Liz. So lonely you talk to yourself. Next comes the dozen cats."

Chocolate chip cookies perfumed the air, bringing Elizabeth to her feet. She'd baked, too. Little activities would chip away at the time. Eat away at the loneliness that inhabited her bones.

Elizabeth padded her way to the kitchen in her college sweats. Laundry-day clothes. Hair piled on top of her head, Elizabeth melted into household details. The everyday tasks that moved a day forward.

Metal sheets removed from the oven with their cookies piping hot and fragrant. With a spatula, she lifted each cookie onto a cooling rack.

A knock brought her domestic bluff to a halt.

Elizabeth opened the heavy, oak door. Corbin was on the doorstep, the van behind him. The passenger window was rolled halfway down despite the chill. A black and white snout breached the confines of the cab.

Arms crossed over paint stains, in that moment, Elizabeth wished she'd done anything but nothing to her hair.

"I came selling cookies, but it doesn't smell like you need my services."

A grin lit Elizabeth's face. "Blame the benzene rings."

"Is that your secret ingredient?"

"Something like that."

Corbin's tone turned serious, and he looked into her eyes. "How are you holding up?"

"I'm...okay. Not looking to go snowmobiling any time soon, though."

"Maybe take up dog sledding?"

Elizabeth enjoyed their banter. She flirted with Corbin, she knew. He was handsome. Smart. Talented at his work, and easy to talk to. But before she could invite him in, her subconscious stopped her. There was the picture with Hannah Black, tucked in his drawer. *Not yet*, she thought. *There will be time to learn more.*

"Care to introduce me to your friend?"

They looked at his truck. The huge husky had muscled a wider window gap and wedged his head through the opening. His long, pink tongue panted, his black, marble eyes watched Elizabeth.

Corbin reached up to scratch the dog between the ears, then patted the metal of the door. "Meet Brutus. Don't let the name confuse you. He's a teddy bear."

Winton's dog. "He's cute. Staying with you now?"

"Actually, he's been adopted. By a rancher. I'm on my way to deliver him to his new home. Help the two of them make sense of each other."

"Good news, then. The others?"

Corbin looked down at his boots, shuffled one foot in the dirt. When he looked up, a wide smile stretched from ear to ear. "Yours truly just secured funding to finish Winton's dream. And the location to do it. Even if I don't finish adopting them out, I'll have no problem expanding my facilities."

"What? That's great! How?"

"Hannah Black. She donated the land on the cliff side. Something about the tax write off."

Elizabeth pursed her lips and nodded. "All about the money. Sounds about right."

"It'll let me expand. Specialize in sled dog rescues, too. Like Winton wanted. Maybe some could be trained emotional support dogs, like Leia and Ranger. Jo's interested and she said you might be willing to help. Maybe you could be on the board of Burro Buddies?"

Elizabeth felt the tears welling. She fought them off and smiled. This is how she would move forward and turn pain into progress. Volunteer her time for dogs that deserved a second shot.

"I would like that."

He reached up to give Brutus another pat. With a wave at Elizabeth, Corbin climbed back into his truck and drove off, the husky's head hanging out the window.

Elizabeth returned to the laundry and left her loneliness on the doorstep. Hope was a pilot light that still burned in her chest.

60

"**W**HAT IS ALL THIS?"

Jo bustled through the door to the dining room, a handful of fork-tipped skewers in one hand. Each had a long, slim handle with a different colored end. "You didn't get to see the race. Or rather, you were the race. So, I thought I'd bring the Swiss chalet experience to you. We've got fondue, rosti, Lekerlis, and Zopf. I was tempted to order in raclette but there's such a thing as too much cheese at my age."

"You've outdone yourself, Jo Wolf. My stomach is growling in anticipation."

Jo nestled the fondue forks into a mug and set them next to a burbling pot on a trivet. A plate laden with sliced sausages, chopped fruits and vegetables, and nuggets of dense, dark bread rounded out the presentation. "I figured we can crack open that bottle of wine you brought and stream last year's Iditarod while we eat. Clint won't be home for hours. By then, we may need the raclette!"

"As usual, you are the best."

"It's nothing. Now if only that brother of yours would show up with the cheese, we could get the party started..."

As if on cue, Casey burst through the front door. In his arms was a big paper sack that blocked the bulk of his face. "Never fear, fair maidens! Emmentaler to the rescue!"

"We hardly qualify as helpless princess types, but we will take that cheese." She lifted the bag from his arms so he could ditch his boots by the front door. "Good grief, did you buy every block of Swiss cheese at the shop?"

Casey jammed his ankle into the boot jack to remove his second boot. "Jo said go big, so I got a couple bricks of Swiss chocolate, too. Oh and some of that English pea salad I like. I know it's not on theme, but I had to have some. It's not every day I make a store run to Billings for the fancy stuff."

"You drove four hours for cheese?"

"And chocolate. But no, I had to pick up some special medicine for one of the goats."

"Add it all to our glorious pile." Jo hummed as she brought out a bowl of marshmallows, then several finger bowls that held a rainbow of sauces. She crossed one arm over her chest to hold up the opposite elbow so she could rest her chin in her hand, considering the spread. After a moment, she snapped once in the air. "The pound cake!"

"I'm gaining weight just looking at this table."

"Burn it off tomorrow, cowboy," Jo said, and elbowed Casey in the ribs "We've got some spectating to do."

After popping a cork, melting the cheese, and loading up their plates, the trio retreated to the couch for an unusual Sunday supper in front of the big screen.

"I can't imagine staying upright in one of those sleds for a day, let alone a week." Elizabeth gaped at the onscreen map of rugged landscape through which the dogs ran.

"It's not 24/7. They do rest." A string of cheese clung to Casey's lower lip. At a signal from his sister, he swiped at it with his napkin. "But you're right. They run them almost a thousand miles."

Jo had moved the fondue pot to the center of the coffee table. Between dunks of speared treats into the rich, creamy mixture, they watched the screen as dog pair after dog pair went by, mushers in hot pursuit of a winning time along the trail.

Outside, the snow picked up. Gritty flakes beat against the windows. Drifts piled up against the buildings. The thick of the storm pressed in on the snug house as afternoon faded into evening.

Earlier, Elizabeth had helped Jo button up the barn with Bessie and Buck safe and snug inside. She wondered what prep would look like at Corbin's facility, the time it would take to get all the animals inside and bedded down.

The tough temerity of the racing canines transfixed Elizabeth's attention on the screen. If she hadn't been around sled dogs, hadn't had the experience of fostering one, she wouldn't know that their personality was so much more than a relentless athlete. The Chinook was something special, a dog bred for the snow, bred for heart. They could be serious workaholics, nose to the ground. They could also be goofy, loving pets. Dogs were incredible creatures, and she wanted more children to have the experience Rhett had.

"I've been thinking about Corbin's project idea." She stabbed an apple hunk with a blue-tipped fork.

"Yeah?"

"What do you think about asking someone like Alma to work with us?"

Casey paused, cramming a cheese-coated apple slice into his mouth. "The film maker?"

"The activist, yeah. I think having someone like her on board would keep us on our toes. In a good way."

"Doesn't she live in Colorado?"

"Fort Collins. We've got video chat now, though, here in the 21st Century. She could help us with messaging, social—communications and stuff like that."

Jo nodded. "I can see that. Let's talk to Corbin."

"Oh, honey, I'm home!" Clint's voice boomed from the front door. "Mind helping me with something out here, Jo?"

"Some days, the guy can barely tie his shoes without me," Jo said in a low voice. She wiped her hands off on a napkin, then called back to him. "Coming!"

Casey and Elizabeth maintained the race watch as the camera followed several teams over a frozen lake. In between obstacles, the broadcast featured champion dogs from the various teams, like basketball player stats on the halftime screen. Along with photographs, weights, and age, each screenshot shared a fun fact about the dog. One only played with cat toys, another loved pears, and the last slept with the same blanket every night.

The now familiar heartache pressed hard at Elizabeth's rib cage. She hoped that wherever Leia was, someone showed her affection, told her she was a good dog.

A thump against the back of the couch was followed by a loud schlep in Elizabeth's ear. The side of her face was in slobber, and she yelped. A bundle of legs and fur leapt into her lap, wriggled with joy, and covered Elizabeth with kisses.

"Leia!"

The dog gave a short woof and spun again to snuggle Casey. Elizabeth put her arms around the dog and surprise turned to laughter and then tears. It was a full five minutes before she recovered enough to turn her tear-streaked face toward Clint. "I don't understand."

"Hannah," Clint said. "She's gifted Leia to you. I have the papers from her lawyer in the truck."

"Seems she has a heart after all," Jo said. She and her husband stood in the doorway, arms around each other, watching joy fill the room.

Elizabeth wiped her face on the sleeve of her shirt. She didn't want to stop petting Leia to use her hands. "Tell her thank you, for me. If you get a chance."

Leia snatched a round of bratwurst off Casey's plate. After a hasty swallow, she panted, tongue lolling.

Casey clutched at his plate in mock annoyance. "Back, foul beast. I'd forgotten what a mooch you are!"

"Hey, she can't help it. Once a snow dog..." Elizabeth set another morsel on Leia's snout. With a quick flip, the disc was airborne a moment before it disappeared between the jaws.

"I think we have a natural fondue fanatic in this one."

61

L EIA, AT HOME IN the fluff, snuffled through the snow in search of a scent. Casey played a gentle round of tug-of-war with Leia using a stick snapped off by the weight of the new powder on the tree branches.

The snow had eased its fall in time for them to slog home from the Wolfs', stuffed to the gills and happy. Elizabeth wore her new snowshoes, a present from Casey that morning. Her brother had wrapped them in shiny, silver paper.

"I know we said no gifts, but it's January and this is actually for me. I could use a workout buddy."

"I love them!"

When they made it inside, thighs burning, they unstrapped the snowshoes while Leia sniffed every inch of the house in search of what she'd missed in her absence.

After she nestled a box of leftover strudel in the fridge, Elizabeth reached into the pantry and withdrew a dish towel-wrapped slab which she handed to Casey.

"What's this?"

"Nothing big. Just something I made for you. For us, really."

Casey unwrapped the package to withdraw a semi-rectangular board, black markings crossing its oiled surface.

"It's the state. There's a heart over Banner, and I used the high school's laser cutter to make the mountain ranges.

"Whoa." Casey ran his hand over the surface. "This is seriously cool."

"It's just a mock-up. For our future plans. I haven't cut the holes for taster glasses yet. Thought you might have ideas about that."

"This is brilliant, Liz. The mountains make perfect nooks for cheeses, nuts, and whatever else we want to pair with the beers. I love it!"

"We've got time to tweak the design. Polish my woodworking skills, too. Meanwhile, we test this sucker out."

Tires crunched on the gravel, and Casey looked toward the window. "Let's do that tonight. I think we've got one more surprise in store for the day."

Elizabeth peeked out the window, then ran to the door and flung it wide open. Nick's SUV sat in the driveway. He extracted Rhett from the backseat and set his son, decked in shiny new boots and a tiny logger hat, down onto the snow.

The little boy clapped once and held his hands up. Before Elizabeth could run to collect him, Leia exploded past her and ran for Rhett.

"Dog! Dog, dog!"

Leia bowled over the little boy and covered him in kisses.

Nick sank to his knees in the snow with a sob and watched the pair, a gloved hand pressed over his mouth.

Elizabeth crossed over to the little group and scooped Rhett into her arms. She left room for Leia to nuzzle under, bestowing appreciative licks anywhere she could.

"He loves her," she said to Nick. She freed a hand to squeeze her ex-husband's shoulder.

Nick shook his head, the tears falling. "I kept hoping he would—but he didn't, and then...oh. It's incredible."

"This is a lovely reunion and all," Casey said. He sniffed and wiped at his own eyes. "But can we head inside? I can't feel my pinky toes."

62

M ID-JANUARY LEFT A FINE, icy crust on the yard. A flock of chickadees ringed Casey's heated bird feeder. He'd hung a pair of suet feeders in the cottonwood. When paired with the warm eaves of the barn and plenty of branches for nests, they'd spotted more than a few species around the house.

Casey headed straight for the shower after splitting logs in the deceptive sunshine. He emerged from the steam-filled bathroom ten minutes later, a towel wrapped around his head.

"I think the Wyoming winter was invented to make us question our own migratory patterns."

"Humans aren't migrational animals. At least not in the traditional sense."

"Exactly. We shouldn't have quit while we were ahead." He sauntered into the kitchen and flicked on the espresso machine. "Want one?"

"Is the pope Catholic?"

Casey filled the reservoir at the sink, then placed it back into the machine. "Hey, speaking of being raised, any news from Nick?"

After Leia's return, then Rhett's, Elizabeth was worn out. The stress of the past weeks had wrung every emotion from her being, and she was left limp and with more questions than answers.

Nick had been quiet. He'd accepted a beer and a night on the couch from Casey. In the morning, he'd packed, then pulled Elizabeth aside. "I can't do this."

"Do what?" Every possible amplification of the awfulness of the last month played through her mind.

Nick pressed his hands together in front of his mouth and closed his eyes. "I can't leave him again and again. I miss him too much."

"Nick—"

"No, let me get this out. I can't take him away, either. Not after what I saw. That dog is a four-legged miracle worker."

"That she is. Put me back together, too. She's family now."

"I need to be closer, Liz." Elizabeth opened her mouth, but he held up one finger and kept talking. "I'm going to see what's available in Billings. Bozeman maybe. Doubt there's anything in Sheridan but I'll look. I can't be this far, Liz. And you can't keep me away."

Leia sidled up to Elizabeth and nudged her hand for pats. Elizabeth complied.

"You're right, I can't. But I can have a say in what it looks like."

"I know. I'll keep you posted with what I turn up."

A week had rolled into two. Elizabeth had tried not to let fear of the unknown take over. She stumbled to get out the words. "No news yet. I expect something, though. He's good at what he does. Someone will want him. The question is when, not if."

"How are you handling this?" Casey rubbed his hair dry, then hung the towel on the doorknob to the tiny laundry room.

Elizabeth watched Rhett drive his brightly colored plastic cars through a model garage. He lay on the tile, tummy down while he played. Leia, chin on paws, observed the amateur mechanic at work. She only lifted an eyebrow when one car used her haunches as its Autobahn.

"I'm okay. For now." Some days, stability is enough to prop us upright.

A soft tap on a horn alerted them to a visitor. Elizabeth spotted the Burro Buddies van through the window. A knock followed a moment later. "I've got it."

Leia followed Elizabeth to open the door. She'd become a watchdog, babysitter, and dinner thief all in one capable pet.

"Hey there," Corbin said. "Casey around?"

"And here I thought you were here to see me." Leia squeezed past Elizabeth to sniff at the van's tires.

The corner of the man's mouth kinked upward. "An added bonus, to be certain. Let me show you why I'm all business today."

Corbin opened the back doors to reveal a small carrier stuffed with blankets. Inside, two kittens who couldn't be more than a handful of weeks old, snoozed in a cozy pile. "Their mama took off after she'd weaned them. Hoping to get some goat milk from Casey to start as a little supplement. Vet says it's okay since they're old enough."

"I'm sure he's got some to spare. Poor little sweeties." Inside the metal pen stretched across the van's cargo area, the two young animals staggered over an oval bed, mewing. "What will happen to them?"

"Barn cats, likely. If I'm lucky. The same guy who took Brutus asked me to keep an eye out for him. Lives just outside Buffalo, and I'm on my way over there."

"Aww, no, they'll freeze to death in a barn!" Elizabeth stroked the round tummy of one of the kittens. The animal rolled onto its side, exposing its belly to the attention.

Corbin stroked the tiny jawline of the other kitten with the edge of his thumb. "Not at this place. Deluxe barn. Heated. Real flooring. The whole nine yards. He got it in a foreclosure of a boarding facility. Killer deal. Even nice barns have mice though, and he needs the help."

"All right, well in that case, let me get my brother," Elizabeth said, stroking a tiny footpad. Its owner flexed its toes in response. "Then I've got something to show you."

"Can't wait."

Elizabeth ducked inside for a moment, then returned. She held a piece of elk jerky pinched between thumb and forefinger. "Leia, here, girl."

Leia ceased sniffing at the kitten crate. She parked herself in front of Elizabeth, eyes on the prize.

Elizabeth moved the treat in a circle through the air twice, as though tracing an elliptical orbit.

Without missing a beat, Leia spun in two neat circles.

"I love it!" Corbin cheered and clapped.

"She's so smart, she practically taught herself. I think she just pretends not to know what I want at first to see if I'll offer food."

Corbin crossed his arms and appraised his friend. "Looks to this semi-professional animal wrangler like you know exactly what you are doing."

Elizabeth grinned. "Maybe I'm starting to figure it out. One trick at a time."

The Dead Swede

1

E LIZABETH BLAU TALKED AROUND the pencil between her teeth, as though it were a rose and her work a tango.

But instead of a paramour whirling her about a dance floor, she wrestled a canopy pop-up with Casey, her brother. Instead of feet stamping a rhythm across a Barcelona stage, he braced himself to boost her upward.

She set one foot in his palm and he lifted as she reached up to press on the crux of their tent poles.

"A little higher," she said, her voice muffled by the pencil.

She half-sat on Casey's right shoulder, one foot pressed into the platform of his hands. Her fingers negotiated a pin above her head that had failed to poke through the designated latch.

With a quick twist of opposing bars, the metal pieces clicked into place. "Got it!"

Casey released her foot, which he'd held while in a squat, and stepped back. She bounced on the balls of her feet when she landed, the memory of cheerleading years taking over.

"Tent, check." Elizabeth removed a twice-folded piece of yellow, lined paper from her back pocket. Pencil now in hand, she consulted the inscribed list and ticked a box with a flourish.

She ducked out from under the canopy to take in the full effect. With the frame in place, blue canvas stretched above, their booth had an official look.

Casey shook out his hands and cracked his knuckles. He brushed at the thighs of his jeans, then pressed on the small of his back. He rolled his neck side to side with a deliberate motion. A cascade of small pops sounded in the crisp morning air. "I need to get back on the mats. Getting older isn't for the weak."

In his prime, Casey was a rodeo champ. He'd gone to college on a wrestling scholarship and picked up roping while in Nebraska. He'd given up the arena lights for a booming goat cheese business.

"I'd hardly call late thirties old. You aren't giving me much hope," Elizabeth said. She reached for her abandoned breakfast burrito. The wrap rested in its crinkled aluminum foil. She'd ordered her and Casey's meal from the cafe that morning. Lukewarm now, the combination of eggs and veggies was still amazing. She took a big bite and chewed. Hot sauce zinged against the roof of her mouth.

"Wait until you get there. Then we'll talk."

"Maybe if you hadn't followed the work hard, play hard mentality to the letter, you wouldn't be such an old man."

Casey laughed. "Easy there. I didn't say I was ancient. Creaky, but not decrepit. Not yet, anyway. How's the list coming?"

"We've got the tent. Two chairs, the table, and the tablecloth. Oh, and this little tin of weighted clips Jo sent. I didn't think we'd need them, but now that I've used some, I may need to get a box of my own." Elizabeth set the list on the table. With a twist of her wrists, she wrapped her hair into a bun and jammed the pencil through its mass, anchoring the hair in place. When a few strands threatened to escape, she added a thermometer from the pile of brewing equipment strewn across the tabletop.

Elizabeth had long hair—for the moment. Half wavy, half straight, she'd grown it out for the ease of braiding and neck warmth in the brutal winter. She told people she planned to donate the length of it. The closer truth was that she wouldn't fork out the money for regular trips to the salon. Couldn't afford it.

Hair in place, list checked, Elizabeth gave a short nod of satisfaction. *This day will go well.*

Casey reached down to pinch one of the weighted clips, each in the shape of a plastic picnic basket. "Huh. Just when you think you don't want to own any more stuff, here comes another invention."

"Pretty sure that's how we ended up with cars and fax machines—and look how far those got us."

"You got me. I definitely appreciate vaccinations and pour over coffee."

Liz scratched at her head with one hand. "Okay. Booth is set up. Tent seems secure. We've still got to claim our token bucket. How about you do that while I set up the coolers and the rest? The entry is under Blau."

"Can do. What about Leia?"

Leia, their newest family member, waited by the corner of their booth space. A big dog, the shade of a sandy beach, Leia attempted patience. Her body remained still, but her tail thumped the asphalt at the mention of her name.

They'd rescued Leia over the holidays. Over the months since, she'd become excited by the hustle and bustle up and down the street. A retired sled dog, she was athletic, eager, and energetic. Her head turned toward each new sound and smell.

"Better take her with you," Elizabeth said. She handed him the leash. "I'm not sure we can trust her around the bratwurst."

The Dead Swede is Book 3 in the Sheridan County Mysteries—order today from your favorite bookseller!

Read the Series!

The Sheridan County Mysteries

The Sheriff's Wife

The New Teacher

The Sled Dog

The Dead Swede
The Master Mechanic—Coming Summer 2023
Reviews help readers find books they'll enjoy and authors find
people who love their stories.
Please consider leaving a review on your favorite bookshop's
website or with Goodreads.

**Subscribe to Erin's newsletter, get a free copy of *The
Sheriff's Wife*, and more at erinlark.com**

Afterword

While this book is a work of fiction, some real people, events, animals, and organizations inspired those found within this story.

Paniolos, Hawaiian cowboys, are talented, hardworking people who for generations have shown their strength and commitment as exemplar livestock experts. In 1908, a paniolo from Parker Ranch on the Big Island, Ikua Purdy, traveled to Cheyenne, Wyoming to compete in a national steer roping championship and won. This is only one example of the rich history of paniolos and the author encourages readers to look into the incredible stories of these inspirational people.

The Bighorn Rush Sled Dog Challenge takes place at the Antelope Butte Mountain Recreation Area near Sheridan around the new year. Athletes, dog and human, race their chosen course two days in a row at the high elevation location for distances of 4-25 miles. While newer than many established sled dog races, this event draws many enthusiasts and follows strict rules and protocols to keep all participants safe while creating an enjoyable atmosphere. If you are interested in sled dog racing, there are many resources for getting to know the sport, ensuring the health and well-being of the animals, and endless fantastic videos of dogs being their wonderful selves.

Chinook dogs are a newer and rarer breed of which the author learned only recently. They are also one of the few, American dog breeds. Their history is tied to the Alaskan

Gold Rush when explorer Arthur T. Walden sought to breed a sled dog that balanced strength, speed, and power with temperament. People have fallen in love with this exceptional dog and they remain a cherished breed. Dog-lovers are encouraged to check out the Chinook Club of America for more on the history of this wonderful breed and the modern day champions of these lovely dogs.

Acknowledgments

I don't know how one can write a book series about family and not be deeply appreciative of one's own kin. A big thank you to my parents who never doubted me and to my sisters who feed my adoration of a quality writing instrument.

Mahalo to Terrilani Chong and Desiree Wright for their knowledge of Hawaiian culture. Thank you for being my teachers.

My warmest appreciation for Patti Richards, the breeder behind Forever Greene Chinooks and the President of the Chinook Club of America for your time, your stories, and the wonderful photographs of a breed worth knowing.

Gratitude to the behind-the-scenes folk: my main editor, Paula Lester, and the creative team at Miblart for their art and their dedication to sending their proceeds back to Ukraine to support the war efforts.

A thousand thank yous to the readers of the Sheridan County Mysteries for being such a fantastic audience. Your kind words, great questions, and fun anecdotes are so precious to me as a writer. Giving you a story worth reading is the least I can do.

Lastly, but most of all, all my love to Bryan and Ava for supporting my late nights at the keyboard with endless hugs and cheer. You two are just the best.

About Erin

From the desert southwest, Erin spent childhood summers along the banks of Piney Creek where she fell in love with Sheridan County. An award-winning science teacher, avid archer, and hack watercolorist, she was made for the out-doors. Erin and her family divide their time between WY, WA, and AZ because life is too short to play favorites.

Follow her on social media @erinlarkmaples

The Sled Dog

Book Two in The Sheridan County Mysteries series

by Erin Lark Maples

Copyright © 2022 by Erin Lark Maples.

All rights reserved.

Cover designed by MiblArt.